Samuel's Daughter

A Love Story
from Third-Century Parthia

ANN BRENER

ISBN: 1-4392-4991-1
ISBN-13: 9781439249918
Library of Congress Control Number: 2009932653

Contents

The daughters of Rabbi Samuel of Nehardea were taken captive and brought to the Land of Israel. They had their captors stand outside and went into the Academy of Rabbi Hanina. One of them said. "I was taken captive but I am unsullied," and the other said, "I was taken captive and I am unsullied." They were declared marriageable. Then the captors entered [to receive the ransom]. Rabbi Hanina said: "They are obviously the daughters of a scholar." Then it became known that they were the daughters of Rabbi Samuel.

(Babylonian Talmud, *Ketuboth* 23a)

Come and hear: Issur the Convert [to Judaism] had twelve thousand *zuz* deposited with Raba. The conception of his son, Rabbi Mari, was not in holiness, though his birth was in holiness, and he was then at school. Raba said, "How can Mari gain possession of this money? If as an inheritance. . ."

(Babylonian Talmud, *Baba Bathra* 149a)

Rabbi Mari, the son of Rachel, Samuel's daughter, related: "On that day I was standing on the banks of the river and saw angels disguised as mariners bringing sand and loading ships with it, and the sand turned into fine flour. When everybody came to purchase it, I called out to them: 'Don't buy this flour because it was produced by a miracle!' Next day, boatloads of rice finally came in."

(Babylonian Talmud, *Ta^{c}anit* 24b)

Prologue

Nehardea, 259 A.D.

Nehardea was in flames. Where rich houses and fine shops once stood, fire now raged, and the cries of the devastated townspeople mingled with the crash of burning columns and the thud of galloping horses. Odenathus of Palmyra and his hordes of wild tribesmen had marched against this proud city on the Euphrates, and in one stroke destroyed centuries of peaceful life and prosperity in the heart of ancient Babylonia. The city that had appeared to the soldiers, as they rode hard across the desert, like a giant grove of date-palms, tender and green, was now a burning conflagration of smoke and fire, and in street after street the neat, whitewashed houses were black with ashes and soot.

Among the soldiers following Odenathus were mercenaries from all parts of the far-flung Persian Empire. One of these, a Parthian archer impatient for his share of the plunder, stood outside the charred remains of what had once been an elegant villa, waiting for a chance to enter and watching idly as a captain of the Horse Guards chained two captives together and placed them under guard. It was very hot, standing there in the sun, and as he waited he removed the helmet from his head and loosened the heavy chain-mail covering the upper part of his body. Soldiers, singly or in larger groups, milled past him through the streets, intoxicated by wine and by war, loaded with plunder and on the lookout for more.

The Parthian looked closer at the captives. They were young girls of fifteen or so, attractive and well-dressed, though covered with soot, and unusually noisy even for captives, rending the air with their cries. Their words were unintelligible to the Parthian, who was only able to make out a few repeating syllables. "Rachel, Rachel!" they cried, over and over again. "Their mother?" the Parthian mused, stroking the ends of his black beard. "Or perhaps the name of their god."

"I wonder," he said to the busy captain, just to make conversation, "that you bother with these two, what with all the noise they're making. Surely there's no lack of captives in this town!" he added, pointing with his helmet to the marketplace, crowded with chained captives of all ages.

The officer paused in his work for a moment and shook his head. "These are rabbi's daughters," he explained. "They'll fetch a good ransom."

Not wishing to appear ignorant, the Parthian said, "Ah!" though he had no idea what a rabbi might be, and was, in fact, hearing the word for the first time in his life.

The two captives were led off, and their cries gradually faded into the distance. Replacing the helmet on his head and fastening it tight against his chin, the Parthian entered the house, which seemed eerily silent and still after the pandemonium of the streets, and looked around him, noting the white marble columns of a spacious atrium and the remains of mosaic on the floor, crushed by the heavy boots of the soldiers. Obviously the home of a well-to-do family, but already picked over by the soldiers, with nothing but broken shards of pottery scattered across the floor, and slivers of glass, blue and green, that shimmered softly in the afternoon light.

Great wooden cupboards were flung open, their shelves gaping and empty, and shreds of rich fabric fluttered mournfully from windows and walls. There would be no plunder in this house. Over in the corner a woman was lying on the floor in a pool of blood, a javelin through her heart; no doubt the mother of those two girls. Disappointed at the lack of plunder the Parthian turned to leave, but just at that moment he heard a noise from the corner near the dead woman. Instinctively raising his spear, he turned - and was surprised to see a little girl. The child looked at the warrior from behind her mother's body, her dark eyes wide with fear. She couldn't have been more than four years old.

The Parthian stared at the child and suddenly knew that this must be "Rachel," the Rachel those girls had been crying for. He continued to stare. The sight of that little girl touched something deep inside of him, made him suddenly long for his own wife and children and feel that he had had enough of war. But what should he do with the child? Just leave her there? He thought with misgiving of the plundering hordes, and hastily rejected that option. There were too many soldiers out there in the streets, and any one of them might yet enter. Bring her to the market-place, to be chained with her sisters? True, the soldier had said they'd be ransomed, but then anything could happen in war.

The Parthian scooped the child up in his arms, and left the house.

Part I

Parthia, the Gurgan Valley, 263 A.D.

Chapter One

The laughter of children rang out deep in the forest. Sunlight filtered through the thick green foliage of towering oaks and the air was still and warm. The slow fullness of summer shed a kind of noontime stillness over the forest, and the children cast about for something to do.

"Let's play Sabbath!" Shirin suggested. "Look, this rock can be the oil-lamp - it's just the right shape - and we can braid these vines into bread, like this, and . . ."

Issur groaned. Already fourteen and hence nearly grown-up, he preferred something more suitable to his advanced years; something more adventurous! "But we played Sabbath just last week," he objected. "Let's play Alexander of Macedon - I'll even be Darius," he added generously. Rustam, Issur's friend from across the village, immediately took up his bow and arrow - a gnarled branch snatched from the ground - and enthusiastically challenged his "Darius." But Shirin demurred. "You know Father doesn't like us to play at that; after all, it wasn't the Dahae who won the war!"

"Since when do you listen to Father?" Issur demanded, exasperated.

"Anyway," Shirin continued, with eleven-year-old scorn and a toss of her hair, neatly braided down her back, "it all happened so long ago; who cares about those things anymore?" She turned to the little girl standing next to her.

"Rachel," she asked, in her big-sister voice, "what do *you* want to play?" Thus appealed to, the little girl lifted dark, almond-shaped eyes and answered just as Shirin knew she would answer.

"Let's play Sabbath," she said.

And that was that. No one ever argued with Rachel, not even Shirin, who was always ready to argue with anyone, even with Father. Not that she always gave in to Rachel with good grace, or refrained from teasing her - that was too much for anyone to ask from Shirin! But over the years, Shirin had learned that there was no point in arguing with Rachel; the little girl cried too easily, and the triumph only made Shirin glum. Issur, as usual, instantly yielded to Rachel's wishes, and Rustam went along with his friend, albeit somewhat reluctantly since it goaded him to let Shirin have her way. He pretended not to see Shirin, who stuck her tongue out at him in triumph.

So the children played the familiar Sabbath game, just as they had played it so many times since Rachel had first brought it to them from across the great mountains. They gathered vines from the thickly-festooned trees and braided them into "loaves," ran into the house to fetch goblets for wine; and here Issur consoled his wounded pride by appropriating Father's best rhyton - the silver one with the fierce stag-head - for his own use. The "wine," of course, came straight from the stream, the children scrambling down the ravine to where it tumbled sweet and clear in a wild landscape of white, lichen-covered boulders shaded by elm trees and ash and an occasional silver-tipped juniper. Up in the leafy oak forest all was still summer, but down here in the ravine there could be no doubt that autumn was on its way, for the leaves of the elm trees were already turning yellow and red, and even the ash was touched with gold. Bird song, which had been stilled up in the oak forest with the stillness of noon, sounded melodiously here amongst the trees, and a deer sipping water from the other side of the brake pricked up its ears for a moment and paused to look curiously at the excited children. Holding onto a branch of the sturdy ash-tree overspreading the stream, Issur cautiously knelt upon one of the slippery boulders, filled the pitcher with clear, flowing water, and then, with a yell, raced Rustam and the others back up the ravine. At this point Rachel took charge of the game, carefully filling the goblets with "wine" and placing the "oil-lamp" and other paraphernalia on a gnarled tree stump; their Sabbath table of old.

The children gathered around, and as they watched in silence Rachel placed her hands over her eyes and mumbled some low words in a language foreign to them all: *Barukhataadonai eloheinumelekhaolam asherkidishanu* . . . the strange-sounding syllables tumbled from Rachel's lips without emphasis, and almost without pause. When Rachel finished, the children each tasted the "bread" and sipped their "wine." Rustam pretended to hiccup, just as he always did at this moment, in order to make Shirin mad. But for once Shirin ignored it. Her thoughts were quite elsewhere, because, for the first time, she found herself wondering what all these things meant, and ignoring Rustam she turned instead to Rachel, who had brought this game with her from across the mountains.

"What, exactly, are you saying when you mumble those strange words?" Shirin asked curiously. "And why do you always cover your eyes with your hands?"

Rachel looked blankly at her sister, surprised by the question. "I don't know," she said. "I just remember that it's what my mother used to do."

"But didn't you ever ask?" Shirin pressed on. "*I* certainly would have!"

"You sure would," Issur agreed, disgustedly. "You always ask too many questions anyway," and Rustam nodded in vigorous agreement. "Anyway," Issur went on, defending Rachel, "she was just a little girl when she came to us. Mother said she couldn't have been more than four!"

Rachel looked like she was about to cry, as she always did when Shirin and Issur argued. So the children changed the subject and raced each other back to the house, Shirin teasing the two boys about this and that, as was her wont. But Shirin's questions had unsettled Rachel, and she hung back from the others as she made her way slowly home.

* * *

At the door, Mother stood waiting to greet her, a tall, slender woman with shining black hair gathered into a knot at the nape of her neck and held in place with a golden hair pin, one of the treasures her husband had periodically brought home from the wars. Like Rachel and Shirin she was dressed in a simple linen tunic - in her case of a somewhat faded pink, for mulberries were common in that part of the valley - loosely bloused over a pair of wide and brightly-colored green trousers, the double-knotted cord worn by all good Zoroastrians wrapped closely around her waist. Though delicately built, Vis was a strong woman, accustomed to farm work, and she held a leathern pail of fresh milk in each hand. From the door of the house she had a good view of the surrounding valley, dotted by wooden houses with neatly thatched roofs and colorful curtains fluttering at the windows. The forested mountain sides stretched just beyond, their jagged slopes covered with richly-grown thickets of oak and elm, and grassy glades in which brown and white cows provided moving spots of color between close wooden pales. In late summer, like now, the fields were covered with clover and wildflowers of every hue, and frisky colts only a few months old raced each other around the enclosure, tails and manes flying past, while the older mares grazed placidly on. It was a beautiful view, peaceful and reassuring; and one that Vis, though born in this same valley, never tired of seeing. Just now, however, she had eyes only for Rachel.

"Well, you're slow today, little one!" Mother smiled, setting the milk-pails down and hugging the child warmly as she came up. "I saw you coming back from the fields, dawdling behind the others. Shirin says you were all playing Sabbath - you never get tired of that game, do you?"

Rachel remained silent for a few moments, looking admiringly up at her mother, for she made a pretty picture against the rough-hewn logs of the house and the leafy apricot trees framing the doorway. She made up her mind to ask her question. "Mother," she said, "What -" and then stopped, for she did not quite know just what to ask her mother after all, or how to put her thoughts into words. She stood silently, absently chewing a strand of hair and thinking intently about what she wanted to say. Shedbez, Issur's horse, trotted up to her, and lowering its head softly muzzled her cheek.

Mother waited for Rachel to finish the sentence, gazing at the girl with fond, loving eyes. She had given her heart to the little girl from the very first, and though she had wondered, in the beginning, where the child came from - what land, what people, and what in the world is a rabbi, Kovad? – she had soon forgotten to care where she came from, or to feel anything but grateful that the gods had given her to them. Shirin, of course, was a joy, but as full as mischief as the day was long and ever eager to be out in the fields teasing the shepherds, or over in the barn playing with the newly-born calves and overturning the milk-pails, or up in the trees or down by the stream, or anywhere, in fact, that her impulsive heart led. Often she was out from dawn until dusk, and it was only Kovad's sterner hand that brought her obediently home for meals or, as she got older, in time for her numerous chores around the house and farm. Rachel, however, was her mother's companion, the daughter who pattered underfoot and played beside her in kitchen and orchard, in barn and field, in sunshine and rain. And yet, for all her loving ways she was not open like Shirin, who loved and hated, teased and pouted, laughed and cried, and never for a moment left anyone in doubt about what she was thinking and feeling. But Rachel was quiet, and, her mother thought, perhaps more complex than Shirin, or indeed than most of the people around her, and when asked what she was thinking she tended to just smile a little, shake her head with an engaging toss of that curly brown hair, and murmur "nothing" in a voice almost too low to be heard. And then go back to looking more pensive than ever.

She was looking pensive now, as she thought about Shirin's questions and the thoughts that were buzzing through her mind. Mother waited patiently, for she never prodded or worried her with questions. But still Rachel hesitated.

So after a while Mother suggested, with a smile, "Why not go on up to the roof? Shirin's up there hulling barley, and Sorhab and Rodoba are there with her. Maybe you'd like to give them a hand before dinner?"

So Rachel climbed the ladder propped up against the wall of the granary a little ways from the house and walked across the flat expanse to where Shirin and two of her friends were sitting cross-legged around a deep wooden bowl and chatting as they worked. Like other families throughout the valley, Kovad grew a little wheat and barley for his own family, just enough to feed his household and provide for the livestock; and the honors of preparation usually fell on the two girls. Hulling barley was no easy task; for the hulls were tough and leathery, and made even the most experienced fingers somewhat raw. But no matter; it was a task they liked; for in good weather they worked up here on the roof and had plenty of company in Shirin's numerous friends, and when it rained or was too cold, they worked in the kitchen, where the hearth fire always burned so cheerfully and Mother could join in their conversation. Neither Rodoba nor Sorhab paid any attention to Rachel as she walked over to them now, but Shirin smiled at her sister and made room for her to sit down even while continuing to listen to Rodoba's story.

Rodoba finished her tale to a gale of laughter from her two friends, and then, eager to prolong the fun, looked mischievously over at Rachel. Rachel's heart bumped in apprehension.

"Remember when Rachel didn't even know the difference between wheat and barley?" Rodoba began, wagging her head in mock dismay. Rachel flushed, even now remembering how the others had laughed at her ignorance in those days long ago.

Shirin rose swiftly to the defense of her little sister, her black eyes snapping with anger. "Well, she knows now - and she's certainly faster than you are; just look at her pile of husks, and you've been up here longer than she has." That was Shirin for you - and Rachel looked gratefully at her sister. But Rodoba and Sorhab seemed bent on teasing today.

"How curly your hair is this afternoon!" Rodoba commented, with a glance at Rachel's tangled locks.

Now, that was a sore point indeed. Shirin, and indeed most of the girls in the valley, had long silky black hair, shining and smooth like pools of deep water. But her! Her hair was brown rather than black, and worst of all, all curls and ringlets, no matter how often she pulled Mother's comb over her head, and this she zealously did every night before going to sleep. For ages now the first thing she had done every morning upon waking was to rush over to Mother's room and pick up the mirror and gaze at herself anxiously in the reflection - surely the curls had been brushed away at last?

"You promised to bring me a potion," Rachel reminded her tormentor.

"Oh, and I will," Rodoba promised. "It's just that I keep forgetting."

Here Sorhab entered the game. "You should have seen Rodoba's hair just last night," she said. "As curly as yours! That potion works wonders."

Rachel had heard all this before, and, as always, she was wracked with anxiety. Were the girls telling her the truth? Or was it all a big joke? She looked over at Shirin, who opened her eyes wide and nodded her head in solemn confirmation of Sorhab's words: even Shirin couldn't resist teasing Rachel in this one little matter - she loved Rachel's curls. She leaned over and gently twirled one of those tangled offenders around her finger, the soft brown strands glinting with red and gold in the sun.

"Well, then bring it tomorrow," Rachel told Rodoba, deciding to give her one last chance.

"Oh, I will," Rodoba replied, and the older girls all burst into peals of laughter.

Offended, Rachel picked herself up and climbed back down the ladder. She found Issur sitting on a log just outside the house, scraping the mud off his boots with the edge of his hunting knife. He looked up as Rachel came in, shoving a lock of hair out of his eyes as he did so.

"Were they teasing you again?" he asked the little girl with a frown. "Don't pay any attention, Rachel, you're prettier than all of them put together."

Mother turned from the hearth, where she was roasting a kid over the fire, her face flushed from the heat and her voice alarmed.

"You mustn't say that, Issur," she remonstrated. "The *daev*s don't like it. Don't you remember the story of Jemshid, who thought he was the greatest king in -"

"Yes, well, I won't say it any more," Issur promised, and then smiled. "But it's true all the same!"

Rachel cheered up - Issur always managed to make her feel better. But the moment nobody was looking she slipped into Mother's room and looked at herself in the little round mirror which Mother kept on the shelf beside her bed, alongside the rest of her treasures. This time she paid no attention to the heavy curling locks or to the little ringlets wisping close to her eyes and across her ears, but instead gazed long and earnestly at the face in the mirror. *Was* she pretty? Issur had said she was, but still, it was hard to say. Shirin, now, was pretty - everyone said so. She examined her face in the mirror: oval shaped eyes and an oval shaped face; nothing at all like Shirin's. Nice enough hair, but - sighing again - those curls! and brown eyes that at times, perhaps, looked black enough, but more often than not almost golden brown in color. A straight nose, rather high-bridged, and a soft but decidedly firm little chin. A wide, well-cut mouth, delicate in line and rich in color. Such was the face that looked back at her in the mirror. Issur had said it was pretty - but how could it be pretty when it looked so different from the other people in the valley? There were no broad cheekbones, and no little tilt at the corner of the eyes to give her that gay, kind of crinkling look that she liked so much in the others, and in her brother and sister most of all.

Rachel put the mirror down with a sigh, and started to leave the room. But as she turned to go her eyes caught hold of the comb lying next to the mirror, the one which she used every night before going to bed. *Then*, her only thought was to tame those curls away, but now she looked at the comb with new eyes, as though seeing it for the first time, and picking it up she turned it over and over in her hands. It was a pretty thing, this comb, carved from some creamy, shining material and encrusted with gleaming stones of a deep, rich red. None of the other girls had anything like it, and Shirin knew that Father had brought it home as a gift for Mother, years ago after some battle. Then she looked down at the mirror: it, too, was a pretty thing; round and shining and decorated on top with a flourish of bronze flowers and fruit, and a snake winding in and out of the foliage. She picked the mirror up again and looked at it pensively, tracing the fine lines of chased metal with her finger. Suddenly she felt a certain kinship with these objects. Like her, they came from far-away. She looked at her face again in the mirror, only this time she was not hunting for beauty. Did she look even a little like Shirin, or like the other girls in the valley? From some angles she thought she did, from others she wasn't sure. She craned her head this way and that, trying to decide.

Mother called her to come and help with dinner and so she replaced the objects on the shelf and went off to perform her chores, now going out to fetch some juniper berries from the trees just outside, now coming in with a basket full of leafy greens and a handful of ripe apricots. The scene up on the roof slipped away from her mind but inside she felt restless and unhappy, churning with doubts and questions. Her thoughts returned to that afternoon in the forest and she pondered Shirin's questions all through dinner and her evening chores, and then as she trailed after Issur towards the barns for a last look at the horses. And she was still pondering them that night when Father gathered the family around the hearth for the evening prayers, stirring the ashes and piling up branches of juniper wood till the flames leaped up brightly. What *did* those strange foreign words mean?

"Come to us as the most joyful, O Fire of Ohrmazd . . ." Father recited the familiar words of the Zoroastrian prayer just as he always did before they went to sleep for the night, but for some reason they were jumbled now in her sleepy mind with the unintelligible words she had murmured earlier that day in the forest.

"We reverence, we requite Thee, O Ohrmazd . . ." Father continued, and now his words mingled not only with the strange words of their game, and with Shirin's questions, but also with the sun and shadow of that dappled forest, till they whirled together in a magical world of blue and green and gold, chasing each other through her thoughts like playful kittens, or like sunbeams behind tightly closed eyes. So greatly did they absorb her that for once she was oblivious to the moment for which she usually waited with breathless anticipation: the moment when Mother and Father ceremoniously untied the sacred cords around their waist, double-knotted in front and back, to recite the *Kemna Mazda*. The children all took special interest in this part of the evening ceremony, especially now that one of their own - the fourteen and a half year-old Issur - was soon to don the sacred cord and become a grown-up himself. Rachel, in particular, always waited for this moment with bated breath. Would the *daevs* strike before they could be retied? Without those knots to protect Mother and Father, she trembled in fear for her family. But tonight her thoughts were elsewhere.

When Mother tucked her into bed that night, the unspoken question hovered on her lips, but somehow she knew that what she had to ask not even Mother could answer. The answers were far away. *Barukhataadonai* . . . "Will I ever find out what those words mean?" she wondered drowsily, just as she dropped off to sleep, but already they were drifting into unimportance, and back into another world.

Chapter Two

Kovad son of Artak, the father of Shirin and Issur, owned his own small farm deep in the Gurgan Valley. The land there was rich and fertile, crossed by numerous streams and surrounded by deep forests full of wild sheep and ibex. His family had lived there as long as anyone could remember, but he knew, as did everyone else in the valley, that their forefathers had come to this fine land from across the Elburz mountains to the east of the Caspian Sea. His own tribe, the Aparni, belonged to the Dahae, whom tradition placed at the Battle of Arbela when Alexander of Macedon fought and conquered the armies of Darius, the Great King of Persia. As though he had fought there himself those many centuries ago, Kovad could name the tribes that made up the left flank of Darius' army, each tribe in its proper order - the Bactrians, the Arachotians, and then the Dahae themselves, mounted on their powerful chargers, bows and arrows stretched taut at the enemy

The Aparni were a proud tribe. From their loins sprang the kings of Parthia, kings who had arrogated to themselves the whole of Persia, scattering the Hellenistic rulers of old like so much chaff in the wind. Even now, when Persia was ruled by a new dynasty who did not know the Aparni, it was a proud heritage to claim. Kovad never tired of listening to the wandering *gosan*s who drifted through the towns and market-places of the valley, strumming their lutes and singing the ancient glories of their people. True, the Parthians no longer ruled, but what did that matter? Carved monuments preserved for all time the brave deeds of the Parthian kings. Who could cross the great desert and not tremble at Behistun, or Sarpul, or Shimbar? And a Parthian mercenary, mounted on his charger and armed with his bow and his quiver of arrows, was still a prize any general would boast to have in his army.

Kovad thought of his family. His wife, Vis, was of the Aparni, too, yet theirs had been a love match, with no arrangement about it. Kovad had married rather late in life, unwilling to give up the roaming ways of a mercenary soldier before he met Vis, and he had never, like some of the richer farmers in the valley, taken another wife alongside her. And yet, even Vis had been unable to keep him at home when the season came to ride off to war. Often, during the winter, when the fields lay still under their burden of snow, the great lords would assemble their farmers to go fight under the banner of the King of Kings, or to serve as mercenaries for some tribal chief across the great mountains.

His thoughts turning to his children, Kovad reflected, and not for the first time, how much his daughter resembled him. Though just a girl, of course, and unable to wander afar as he himself had done in his younger years, he sensed in Shirin that same fearlessness, the same longing for adventure and change. But naturally she would marry and settle down young, far younger than he himself had done, indeed probably quite soon. That Shirin would marry Rustam, the eldest son of a prosperous farmer there in the Gurgan Valley and a former comrade-in-arms, Kovad had not the slightest doubt. The kind of bickering that went on between Shirin and Rustam, young as they were, could lead to only one thing!

Issur, on the other hand, was like his mother. Strong and sturdy, eternal like the mountains and rocks. He would no doubt marry Rachel, Kovad thought, and the idea did not displease him; indeed quite the contrary. She might not be of the Aparni - indeed Kovad had no idea *who* her people might be - but she was as good to him as a daughter, and Issur loved her with all the strength of his young heart. Anyone could see that.

Kovad sighed in contentment. The gods had been kind to him. His farm was rich and well-tended; his land protected by high sheltering mountains; his horses and cattle blessed with good pasturage. His children would marry and carry on the traditions of their people. Fields would be tilled, wars would be fought, grandchildren and great-grandchildren born and raised. Such, of course, was the way of the world, but still, the gods deserved thanks for their blessings. The feast of *Nauruz* was approaching, and he would not forget to offer up his thank to Ohrmazd, who had granted him so much. And when he died, as someday he must, his body would be left to the wolves and the ravens upon his ancestral fields, to be reunited into the cycle of all creation. That, too, was the way of his people.

Chapter Three

It was market-day. From all across the valley farmers rode into Astarabad astride spirited horses, eager to purchase goods for their households and farms, meet with old friends, and discuss the news of far-off events. In this remote area of the Gurgan Valley market-day came but once a year, and for the children it was as good as a holiday. Even Shirin, normally rebellious and less than mindful of her mother's orders, behaved with exemplary obedience in the weeks just before market-day, lest she be forbidden to ride into town with Father and Issur. Rachel, riding her chestnut mare between Shirin and Issur on this beautiful spring morning, was not quite as eager, but even she felt the mounting excitement of the crowds and the noise as they drew closer and closer to the site of all the commotion.

This year the market was even more crowded than usual. After tethering their horses under the sprawling oaks and exchanging words with their neighbors, the family separated to go their different ways, Father and Issur to make the rounds of the horse-dealers and to purchase bridles and leather bits, Shirin and Rachel to make purchases for Mother, who was ill this year and unable to join them. Shirin loved going round the different stalls to see the various wares for sale, running her fingers over delicately chased silver ewers from Susa, and gazing hungrily at shimmering silks from India and China. She admired beautiful cut-glass bowls from Media and purchased little oil-lamps in glazes of blue and green, flecked with yellow and brown. As usual, she paused at the booth selling the death-defying feathers of the great Varagna-bird, and tried to bargain with one merchant for butter in alabaster jars, but, also as usual, the merchant held firm. Why, the tax alone on a camel-load of these jars cost twenty-five drachmas, nearly twice the amount for butter stored in skins. Rachel followed along timidly, but Shirin loved the color and the noise and the bright excitement of the whole scene. How dreary everything always seemed back at home, after market-day!

The girls finished their purchases, packed them on the horses, and then, since there was no sign of either Father or of Issur, went back to strolling amongst the crowds, nibbling *gozaz* and looking at the brightly-colored displays of handiwork. By now Shirin had become the center of a lively group of chattering girls, and arm-in-arm with Maneza, her special friend, they all lingered over a display of gold and silver jewelry. Shirin tried on a bracelet, pushing the delicate silver band up her arm, and the girls just had time to admire the fine ibex-heads carved in gold at the tips, the strong horns curled fiercely back, before the merchant shouted at Shirin to take the thing off. Laughing, she did so, and turning away came face to face with a merchant offering an array of creams and lotions in small glass vials; one of them, he assured the girls, containing a rare unguent that came from the treasure-chest of the great King Darius himself, and was made of nothing less than lion's fat and saffron, with just a touch - just a pinch - of palm oil and gum laudanum. With a look of importance, Shirin sniffed at the sample held out for her inspection, made a face that set her friends giggling, and swept off to the next booth with the girls in her wake. But for Rachel, trailing alone at the edge of the group, all the fun had gone out of the day.

With Shirin arm-in-arm with Maneza, and the center of a blazing comet of girls, Rachel felt awkward and alone; out of place amidst the crowds and unable to catch the sense of joyousness that apparently filled everyone else. She had a disheartening sense of being alone, and though this feeling was not unfamiliar to her, today it was unusually strong. Why did this always happen, she wondered? Every year it was the same: every year the same anticipation; every year the same let-down. And not only at market-day: the Zoroastrian calendar was filled with holidays and feast-days of all kinds, for penance and gloom were no part of Ohrmazd's creation. Only she, and she alone, as it seemed to her, was unable to rejoice along with the others, and she was overwhelmed by the feeling that in some way, some mysterious way that she could not define, she was different from the others. Rachel looked over at Shirin, but Shirin had her head next to Maneza's and snatches of their conversation came drifting back to her. Apparently they were discussing preparations for the village banquet next week in honor of *Nauruz*, the New Year.

"I don't know," Shirin was saying, rather doubtfully. "I brought seven twigs of seven flowers last year, and seven kinds of colored pebbles the year before. I'm really beginning to run out of sevens."

"Seven kinds of cheese?" Maneza suggested. But Shirin shook her head. They passed near a stall in which finely-worked bridles and bits, beautifully embroidered, were displayed in colorful profusion, and amongst the men clustering around them Maneza caught a glimpse of Issur. She nudged Shirin's arm in his direction.

"Too bad you don't have seven of *him*," she said, laughing rather ruefully. "The one you have only has eyes for Rachel." Shirin looked around, to make sure that Rachel was still with them. She saw her trailing behind, and catching Rachel's eye and giving her a loving smile, she looked back at Maneza and nodded cheerfully, as though to say, "Well, what could you expect?"

In the center of the market a large crowd had gathered and was laughing good naturedly at something the girls were unable to see. "What is it?" Shirin asked, plucking at the sleeve of a farmer. "Shh . . ." the farmer answered back, "it's the *gosan*." The *gosan*! The girls edged nearer until they were able to see, and Shirin left Maneza to link arms with Rachel. It wasn't often that one of these wandering minstrels came their way. How often they'd heard of the great Barbad of Marv, whose fame reached even the smallest villages in the deepest valleys of Parthia. The *gosan* performing just now was a young man dressed foreign-style in a short silken tunic and sandals that laced up his bare legs, and unlike the Parthian men, who wore their hair long and tied back, his hair was short and his forelock blew freely in the wind. He stood on an overturned wagon, amusing his audience with a song about a billy-goat and a palm-tree, accompanying his words with extravagant gestures that made his audience burst into laughter. The two girls laughed with them, enjoying the way the *gosan* skillfully played both roles, becoming first the sassy billy-goat and then the haughty palm-tree, each boasting in turn of its own virtues. Which would prove superior to the other? The girls craned their heads to see.

Then someone stepped on Shirin's foot and brought her attention back to earth. It was Issur.

"Can't you be careful?" Shirin asked crossly. "You nearly broke my toe."

"Father's looking for you two," Issur informed her. "He's saddling the horses and is ready to go back."

"We'll be right over," Shirin sighed, glancing with regret at the laughing crowd and turning to follow Issur. But Rachel stood mesmerized by the *gosan*, oblivious to Shirin and everyone else. The *gosan* had begun a new song, accompanying himself on his lute, and the crowd grew quiet. This song was different, very different from the other one. Its words were difficult to understand and somehow evocative of far away places and long ago times. Rachel listened, transfixed.

When I was but a lad, at home in my father's palace
and delighting in the joys of life in Hyrcania
my mother and father gave me great treasures and bade me
go forth, with gold from Carmania and silver from Gazak,
with rubies from India and white opals from Kushan.
And they made a covenant with me,
inscribing it upon the walls of my heart lest I forget, saying:
"Thou must go down unto Egypt and bring back the pearl
which lies fathoms deep in the heart of the sea -"

"Rachel!" Shirin called to her, surprised at the delay. But Rachel was unable to tear herself away, and the *gosan* continued his song:

. . . the road was long and hard
and I was all alone, so very young to travel it.
I crossed the borders of Mesene
where the merchants of the East assemble,
and reaching the land of Babylonia I entered -

"Rachel!" she heard again, this time in the deep, obviously irritated voice of her father. She turned away, sighing. What would become of the young prince? Would he ever find this marvelous pearl? And what was a pearl, anyway? Perhaps Mother would know; Mother knew so much, so many songs and stories. She thought about the *gosan*'s song all the way home, unusually quiet on the journey, but that night, when her mother pulled the blanket over the pallet she shared with Shirin, the questions rose to her lips - and then died there unasked. She never did ask her mother, neither that evening nor the next, nor all the evenings thereafter. But she did not forget the *gosan*'s song.

* * *

The rainy days of late spring set in, and the two girls were confined to the house more often than Shirin, at least, would have liked. But there was always plenty to do about the house, and one morning Mother set the girls before the kitchen table and put them to the yearly task of polishing the various stone vessels used throughout the house and farm. The vast sky itself was made of stone, and polishing these utensils, keeping them shining and clean, was one way of honoring Khshatrya, the guardian of the heavens in all their purity. Saving the sacred pestle and mortar for last, the girls busied themselves with pots and pans and other household utensils, and even Shirin rubbed away with good will. The rain beat pleasantly against the windows and for a while, all was quiet. Issur and Father were still sleeping, having come in late last night from a long journey to the east to purchase horses and cattle. Then, with a gust of wind and rain, The door opened and Issur walked into the room, soaked to the skin and his black hair plastered damply to his forehead. Rachel and Shirin looked up, surprised.

"Why, what were you doing outside?" Shirin asked. "We thought you were asleep."

Issur shook his head, moving over to the blazing hearth and stretching his hands out to the fire. "Been up for hours. I wanted to check up on the horses we brought in last night - make sure they had been properly rubbed down and fed." He paused, and then looked a bit shyly at Rachel. "There's a fine mare that will do for you."

Rachel looked up, pleased, but Shirin, with fine sisterly scorn, said, "You're dripping all over the place," and ordered him to close the door. Issur pulled the bench away from the wall, and seating himself at the table across from the girls told them all about the journey into Bactria across the steppes to the east. He described the vast stretches of rolling land and the thickets of almond and pistachio trees that grew along the way; evidence of which now lay in the burlap sacks piled high in the corner of the kitchen. Shirin rose to bring Issur something hot to drink, rummaging for a few pistachios along the way, and while she was gone Issur took the opportunity to say a few private words to Rachel. He walked over to the corner of the room where his knapsack had been dumped with the rest of the sacks last night, and taking something out of it he said, "Look, Rachel! I brought you this," and set a large piece of jagged rock on the table before her. The rock was unlike anything she had ever seen before; silver-white in color, and seemingly transparent, but when Issur held it up to the light it flashed with all the colors of the rainbow. Rachel caught her breath at the beauty of the shimmering thing. "What is it?" she asked softly.

And then Shirin came back and she, too, asked, "Why, what's that, Issur?"

"*Apakenak*," he informed them. "Rock-crystal. Or, at least, that's what they call it in Bactria. It's all over the place there, and the locals say that they're pieces of the sky. And," he continued thoughtfully, turning the rock around and around in his hands to catch the light's rays, "who knows but what they're not right?" Rather awed at the idea, and subdued into silence, the three of them sat gazing at the beautiful object till Shirin laughed a bit and brought them back down to earth.

"Just like a man," she declared, "to bring something else that needs polishing!"

They all laughed at this, but then Issur added, "No, this will never need polishing," and handed the rock-crystal to Rachel. "It's yours," he said, smiling. Blushing, she accepted the gift with both hands and set the beautiful rock down on the table before her. They continued to gaze at it, still affected somehow by the shining beauty of the thing, despite their laughter of a few moments ago. It was as though a piece of the sky really had fallen into their midst.

Unusually, Rachel was the first to break the silence. "It makes me think of the *gosan*'s song," she said. "You know, Shirin, the one we heard a few weeks ago, just before leaving the market-place." And she quoted softly: "Inscribing it in my heart lest I forget, saying: Thou must go down to Egypt and bring back the pearl, which lies in the heart of the sea.'"

"But this isn't a pearl," Shirin answered pragmatically. "And Bactria isn't Egypt."

"No," Rachel agreed, mulling over her thoughts, and then looking up at the other two. "But I don't think that was what the *gosan* meant. I don't think he really meant Egypt, but just some place far away and unknown. And I don't think he really meant a pearl. Or at least not a real pearl," she added, for now she knew all about these treasures of the sea, having sounded the village elders for the information she needed. "I think he was talking about something else altogether. Something that is inside of us, but which maybe we have to go away to find. Our *inner* being." Shirin looked away, distinctly ill-at-ease with this kind of talk, but Issur looked interested.

"Like the *Daena*, you mean?" he asked. This was a reference they all understood, having heard since earliest childhood of the spirit that accompanies the dead across the Chinvat Bridge, and that appears in the form of either a lovely maiden or an ugly hag, all depending on whether the deceased had had good or evil thoughts and deeds during his or her lifetime.

But Rachel shook her head. "No, not the *Daena*. If the *Daena* is made up of our own thoughts and deeds, she has to be inside of us in the first place. No, I think the *gosan* was talking about something else; something that is *lacking* inside of us, something *here*," she explained, touching her breast in the earnestness of her desire to explain her ideas, "and about the need of going to find it."

"But why should we have to go away to find it?" Issur argued, somehow uncomfortable with the idea of anything that connected Rachel with far-away places. "It's the same sky above us all, and the same earth beneath our feet, for all that in some places we find these rocks," he said, nodding towards the gift he had given Rachel, "and in others we don't - it's all ruled by Ohrmazd and the same *yazad*s."

Rachel listened respectfully, but was still not convinced. "I still think that's what the *gosan* meant," she said firmly.

"Well, if he did," Issur said shortly, "*I* think he was wrong." Suddenly they both noted that Shirin had disappeared, and they laughed a little at the finesse with which she had slipped away from the conversation. And now they noticed that the rain had stopped and that the sun was shining, splashing the walls of the room and the oaken table and benches with even brighter rays of color than the rock-crystal had done.

Shirin poked her head through the window, rain-drops glistening in her hair. "Rachel, you should see your mare - she's a beauty!"

"What color is she?" Rachel asked with interest, glancing at Issur with a shy smile at the same time.

"White. White with -"

"With yellow ears and a golden muzzle?" Rachel said, completing Shirin's sentence with the words from a hymn they all knew, and turning a mischievous smile at Issur.

"The golden muzzle will come later," Issur assured her, pushing the bench away from the table. And getting to his feet he looked down at Rachel, and with a smile that was only half joking he said, "Well, all I know is that if, when it comes time for me to cross the Chinvat Bridge, my *Daena* looks even a little like you - I'll be happy."

Chapter Four

Years passed, till no one could even remember a time when Rachel had not been part of the family. Shirin was now eighteen, Rachel - deemed by common consent some two or three years younger - and hence fifteen or so, and Issur almost twenty, a proud warrior well-schooled in the arts of war. When he came home from his first campaign, full of stories and tales of martial valor, Rachel fixed her large brown eyes on him and drank in every word. But Shirin just scoffed. "If *I* were a man . . ." she'd say meaningfully, leaving Issur to discover his deficiencies on his own. Fortunately for her, however, Issur had eyes and ears only for Rachel. But Rustam, Issur's comrade-in-arms, was not so lucky. Just as Kovad had confidently predicted, Rustam was head over heels in love with Shirin, and husband and wife looked forward to the time, surely not too far away, when the two would marry and give them their first grandson. The families were in agreement, and Shirin's dowry of silver coins stood ready. Shirin, however, refused to hear a word on the subject. "Oh, I'll marry him of course," she told Rachel confidentially, "but he doesn't have to know that - at least, not right away!" And in the meantime she thought of ever new ways to exasperate her love-stricken swain.

One day, when Issur and Rustam were practicing their archery out in the forest together with some of the other young men from the valley, Shirin and Rachel interrupted their chores to go out and watch. Standing in the shadows of the great oaks, the two girls absently stroked the horses which the young men had tethered to the trees, and watched as they took turns aiming their bows at distant targets. None of the young warriors acknowledged the girls' presence, but when Rustam took his turn and hit the target squarely in the center, he couldn't help flickering his eyes in Shirin's direction, practically inviting her admiration. But Shirin just laughed and shrugged her shoulders. "Practice makes perfect!" she said loud enough for all to hear, and then daintily made her way back to the house as Rachel, somewhat appalled, ran behind her.

After this it was open warfare. Rustam refused to greet Shirin whenever their paths crossed, or even to look her way. Shirin pretended not to care, but since there was no one she enjoyed teasing quite as much as Rustam, she eventually fell to planning ways that would force him to make up with her. After all, the feast of *Nauruz* was approaching, and even the great King of Kings made peace with his enemies at this time. She discarded first one idea and then another. Finally, remembering an old story that her mother used to tell them, she hit on the answer to her problem. "Come with me!" she said one morning to Rachel, and dragged her out to the fields.

During the night one of the cows had calved, and as the mother-cow mooed angrily at the girls, Shirin, much to Rachel's surprise, picked up the new-born calf, brown and white and loudly bawling, and walked around with it in her arms. "What are you doing?" Rachel asked in astonishment, but Shirin just continued walking around the shed for another ten minutes, before giving the calf back to its indignant mother. "Now Rachel," Shirin warned her sister, "don't tell anyone about this." Thereafter, every day for two months, Rachel accompanied Shirin to the fields and watched curiously as Shirin picked the growing calf up in her arms and walked with it around and around. The calf's mother, now indifferent to these strange goings-on, lazily watched and munched grass.

Two months passed in this fashion. Then one day, when Shirin knew that Rustam and Issur would be nearby, she took Rachel by the arm and ran out to the field to perform her usual ritual. Rustam, who was leaning against the fence with Issur, and talking with a group of neighboring girls on their way to bathe in the stream, was unable to hide his astonishment as the slender young girl picked up a two-month old calf and carried it around in her arms. The girl looked at him and announced, "Practice makes perfect!" and in the ensuing laughter Rustam condescended to forget his grudge.

The other girls crowded around Shirin. "How did you ever think of that ruse?" one of them asked curiously.

"Oh, it's from a story that Mother told us long ago - remember it, Rachel? It was about the Princess Gurdoya, and so I thought, what works for the princess will work for me!" Everyone laughed again, and looked at Shirin with admiring eyes.

The girls then made their way over to the stream, for the day was hot and the cool water would be doubly welcome. Shirin led the way, the center of a knot of eagerly chatting girls. Rachel turned to one of her friends in order to tell her the entire story of the wayward princess, just as she and Shirin had heard it from Mother, but the girl listened indifferently and soon made an excuse to catch up with the other girls crowding around Shirin. Rodoba - she of the magic potion, who used to tease Rachel about her curly hair - edged closer to Rachel, and Rachel smiled at her, grateful for the attention. But Rodoba was not in a friendly mood.

"I suppose you'll be thinking up some trick like that soon, to make Issur notice *you*," she said spitefully, and then swept away with the others.

Tears sprang to Rachel's eyes. She knew very well that Rodoba was jealous, and that she, Rachel, had no need to think up anything to attract Issur, but still, she was stunned at the sheer meanness of the remark. What had she done to deserve it? Left to herself, Rachel trailed behind the laughing crowd and sat down on the gnarled stump of a great tree that had been blasted by lightening, watching pensively from a distance as the girls splashed each other from the banks of the stream, laughing and talking as they played in the bright sunshine.

A butterfly lit upon her hand, mistaking the girl for a wildflower, and then, disappointed, flew away. Rachel's eyes followed the bright colors flitting upwards towards the sun, like the strands of the rainbow-colored silk the girls wore during the feast of *Tiragan* and then sent sailing into the sky. Long after the other girls had turned their eyes back to earth in gay banter and song, Rachel's eyes would follow the bright silken strands till they could no longer be seen. Why, she now wondered to herself, why was she always the one who was different? Why was she always the one left on the sidelines, or standing silent and stiff in the midst of the crowd? Ever since she could remember, the village girls had teased her for this very reason and mocked her for being so different from them. Some of the girls had even taken to calling her "Tush" and mockingly prostrating themselves before her, pretending to believe that Rachel was in truth the goddess Tushnamati, the divine being who ruled silent thought. Shirin, of course, never mocked her, and certainly did all that she could to protect Rachel from such witticisms, but still, there was no denying that she was different even from Shirin. When the girls drew water from the river, it was always Shirin who splashed and dunked - and got dunked in return - and Rachel who gazed into the watery depths and wondered whence they came. Or if out milking the cows, it was Shirin who cajoled them into giving their milk, who sang her songs to the world at large, and Rachel who looked deep into the cows' soft brown eyes and wondered what they were thinking. It had always been like that. But now, for the first time, she began to wonder: why? And in fact, a number of questions began going through her head, all of them adding up to one big question that was both "why?" and "where" and "how" and many other things at one and the same time.

She plucked the grass with a meditative hand. Why was she so different? Why did she always feel out of place, unable to share what others seemed to be feeling, thinking, experiencing? And all of a sudden, she thought: maybe it was because she came from somewhere else? Maybe it was only *here* that she was different? Maybe, in some other place, she would be more like the other girls, less pensive and plodding, more spontaneous and gay. More like Shirin, in fact! Once she had told Issur that she wished she were like Shirin, only to have him shake his head with good-humored horror. "One Shirin is quite enough!" he had replied, with sham terror at the idea of another Shirin on the loose. But now, reaching back into her memory as far as she could go, it seemed to her that she remembered a little girl who had once been - her; a little girl who was always running around and getting into scrapes; a little girl with curly brown hair who was always busy and happy and full of plans for the morrow. Surely that was her, the real Rachel?

Rachel was fifteen, now, perhaps even sixteen, and she knew a great deal about the world around her. She knew, for example, that the sky was a precious stone that surrounded the earth, and that the sun flew in and out of the three-hundred-and-sixty windows of Harat - the highest mountain peak in the world, taller than the sun and the moon and the stars - and that it was this which created night and day. And she knew that Ohrmazd, who was good, was in perpetual warfare with Ahriman, who was bad, and that it was this which made the world the place it was: a place of dark and light, of cold and heat, of truth and lies, of love and hate. She was not naïve; she knew perfectly well that there was nowhere on earth - apart from the blessed realms of Hukairya, that is, high above the peaks of Harat - where life was ideal and where ills of all kinds had been banished. But still, might there not be *some* place on earth, some other place where things were more . . . more balanced, where there was less of spite and less of hate, and more of warmth and love? Some place where she would fit in better, and feel that she belonged? After all, what was she, in truth, but a stranger here?

"Rachel!" a voice called across the fields. It was Mother, and Rachel woke from her reverie with a start, flushing with shame at her thoughts. How could she even think of any place but this? They had treated her as a daughter from the first. Issur, back in the early years, had pummeled any boy who referred to her as a slave, and Shirin had always been swift to defend her against the village girls and whatever snide comments they might choose to make about her, or about her origins. Captives were not always so lucky, she knew. Darin, for example, who lived on the neighboring farm, had also been brought from far away as a child, a captive of war, and though treated well she did not live with the family but in a little shed behind the cow-byre. She had, moreover, been branded. But she, Rachel, was treated as a true daughter of the house.

She supposed she would marry Issur in a few years, just as Shirin would marry Rustam. The idea did not displease her, and in her imagination she saw the years stretching before her like a quiet green valley, rich and fruitful, and sheltered from the rough mountain winds. Rachel knew that Issur loved her with all the strength of his proud young heart. And of course she loved him, too; how could she not? But somehow, something inside of her yearned for something different; something that she herself could scarcely define. Only, it made her feel like a traitor to admit it, even to herself.

Chapter Five

The Feast of *Mihragan* fell in mid-autumn at the height of the harvest season. After the evening chores were finished the young men of the valley climbed the hilltops to light large bonfires and the unmarried girls gathered around the crackling piles of timber, munching fruits and nuts and watching as the flames danced and whirled in the cool autumn air, making the familiar scenery somewhat eerie and mysterious. Later, one of the old warriors would ascend his rooftop and call out "O ye angels, come down to earth, strike the *daevs* and evil-doers and expel them from the world," but right now the girls were gathered around Artadukht, the best story-teller in the village, and listening to the sad romance of Ardashir, King of all Persia, and the daughter of King Artabanus.

". . . and," Artadukht told her hushed audience, "she surpassed in beauty the cypress, the moon and the rose. But that night, when he took her, the prince discovered that a rose petal, pressed against her cheek, had bruised the young girl. He questioned her, saying 'How, then, have you nourished this body of yours, that it should be hurt by a rose?' The girl cast down her eyes and replied, 'My parents fed me on the marrow of ewes, on honey produced by young bees, and on pure wine.' Astonished, he exclaimed -"

What the young prince exclaimed the village maidens were destined not to hear, but on this point they were not too troubled - for they all knew the story by heart anyway.

For just as Artadukht was reaching the high point of her story, two tall figures emerged out of the twilight on the edge of the forest, and pausing at some distance before the bonfire looked curiously at the festive scene before them. Strangers! Shirin brightened immediately and hand in hand with two of her friends, walked up to the men to welcome them.

As the girls approached the men made a low bow, and then straightening up, the younger and taller of the two met them with a smile. "Ah," he said, "you come to us like the girls in the ballad, the ones who welcomed the King with songs of royal wars when he entered the forest disguised."

"Oh!" said one of the girls, "are you then the King?"

"No," he replied with another smile, "just that the welcome is royal."

Shirin studied both men. They were dressed in the tunics and trousers usual to men in these parts, though there was no double-knotted cord around their waists, and their knee-high boots were red in color and apparently of unusually fine quality. Both men spoke Persian well, but with a strong foreign accent with which she was unfamiliar. "Perhaps then you are *gosans*?" she said helpfully. "You seem to be wanderers."

The older man looked somewhat startled and replied, "No, not wanderers by profession, just lost at the moment. We are merchants on our way to Syria, but have somehow become separated from our caravan. If you could but point out the direction to Damghan, we can probably catch up with the other riders as they encamp for the night."

The girls explained the direction which the strangers must take, and then hospitably invited them to share their feast before setting off again. The two men hesitated, gracefully thanking them for their kind offer but declining to partake of any refreshment. They pointed to their bulging knapsacks filled with provisions, and accepted only some water dipped fresh from the stream.

"What are you merchants of?" Shirin asked inquisitively, loathe to permit such a welcome diversion to vanish so soon again into the forests. Newcomers were a rarity in these parts. "Where do you come from, and where are you going? And how did . . ."

The younger man laughed. "We are returning from China," he told her. "We are part of an embassy that sent His Majesty, the Emperor Wu-Ti, ostrich eggs and jugglers from Petra. His Majesty," he added modestly, "was most pleased to receive them, and in return has given us beautiful silks which we will sell in the markets of Babylonia."

"Babylonia," Shirin mused, softly repeating the word to herself. "I have heard of it. Is it near Mesene, or Kushan?" she asked, recalling names she had heard Father mention. The younger of the two merchants laughed at her ignorance, but his companion answered the girl's question with due gravity. "Babylonia, which the Chinese call Ta-to'in, is situated on the western side of the Great Sea. Its territory covers several thousand *li*, and it contains over four hundred cities. It has much gold, silver, and precious stones - coral, amber, glass - and gold-embroidered rugs of various colors. They also have a fine cloth called the 'down of water sheep,' which is made from the cocoons of wild silkworms. All the precious things of land and water make their way to the markets of Babylonia, from the gems made of rhinoceros horn to chrysoprase, serpent pearls and asbestos cloth." The girls were properly awed to hear of such riches.

"Is it dangerous to travel there?" one of them asked.

The merchant considered the question. "No it is not particularly dangerous," he answered, "once you round the sea and turn northwards. Caravans are not usually attacked by robbers, but the road can become unsafe with fierce tigers and lions."

"Then why don't you travel by sea?" Shirin asked curiously. She herself had never yet seen the sea, but she had heard much about tides and storms, waves and sea-monsters, and it greatly appealed to her imagination.

"The sea is vast and great," he replied, "and with favorable winds it is possible to cross within three months. But if you meet with slow winds, it can also take you two years. For this reason, those who go to the sea take on board provisions for at least three years." The merchant hesitated a moment and then added, "There is something in the sea which is apt to make a man homesick, and several, I hear, have thus lost their lives . . ."

The girls grew silent, each of them pondering the merchant's words and wondering what it would be like to be lost at sea, so far from home. After a few moments the merchants broke the silence to thank the young girls for their kind welcome, and turned to go. "Wait!" said Shirin. "My sister and I will show you the right path. Rachel!" she called imperiously.

The girls dispersed, and Rachel, who had stayed behind at the fires, came shyly up to Shirin and the two men. To the girls' surprise, the two men stood rooted to the spot, staring pensively at the young girl who had just joined them.

"Rachel," said one of the men, tentatively. "That's an unusual name for a Parthian girl."

"Yes," agreed Shirin, pleased that they had noticed. Of course, neither Shirin nor anyone else in the village ever thought of Rachel as anything but a member of Kovad's family, but just now Shirin was proud to claim membership, thanks to Rachel, to the greater world to which these men clearly belonged.

"She's your sister?" the man repeated, still looking at Rachel. Rachel herself stood silent, her eyes cast shyly down. Shirin answered for her as a matter of course.

"Yes, my little sister."

"How old is she?" the other one asked.

"We don't know exactly," Shirin answered, somewhat surprised by the question. "She came to us when she was just a child. Though she could already speak a strange language . . . *barukhatadonai el . . . el* . . . oh, I don't remember the rest. But she could say it all, and very fast, even then."

The men looked at each other for a silent moment. Then the older one turned to Rachel and addressed her directly. "Where did you come from?" he asked her. Rachel remained silent, her eyes fixed on the ground.

He tried again. "What was your father's name?" But Rachel still refused even to look up.

The men hesitated. There was an uncomfortable silence, and after a few moments Shirin stepped into the breach. She was beginning not to like the conversation, and to wish the men well on their way back to their caravan. "She doesn't know," she told the two strangers, almost haughtily. "She was just a kid. And anyway, she . . ." But to her surprise, her words were interrupted by Rachel. Rachel, whose voice was rarely heard in public, and who never addressed strangers, now lifted her eyes and spoke.

"Samuel," she said, slowly. She was gazing straight at the two men, but she did not, in reality, see them at all. Her eyes widened, as though puzzled by her own answer, and when she spoke again there was a touch of wonder in her voice. "Samuel," she repeated more firmly. "His name was Samuel."

Part II

Nehardea, 272 A.D.

Chapter Six

Nehardea, the ancient city, lies in the bend of the Euphrates, doubly protected from its enemies by the steepness of its embankments and by the thickness of its walls. Know - as the blessed sages of old tell us - that when Israel was exiled to Babylonia, the nobles of Judea were brought to Nehardea, where they built houses and planted gardens and raised families, as commanded by the prophet Jeremiah. There, in this rich land of grain and wine, King Jehoiachin himself helped build a synagogue on a foundation of stones and earth which he and his nobles had brought with them from the Holy Temple in Jerusalem. This synagogue they called *Saf ve-Yativ*, that is, that the Temple "traveled and settled" there.

And there the Jews settled, too. In time they learned to take pride in their new home and to recall all its ancient claims to glory. Were not the Tigris and Euphrates two of the four rivers of Paradise? Was it not from these lands that God had scooped up the dust for Adam's body? Why, Abraham himself came from Babylonia! Yes, Babylonia was very great indeed.

If, in the days of Cyrus, the Jews of Babylonia did not heed the call to return to the Land of Israel, neither did they forget their ancient homeland. It was from the city of Nehardea that the half-shekel paid by Jews everywhere flowed towards the coffers of the rebuilt Temple in Jerusalem, guarded by the tens of thousands who made the yearly pilgrimage to the land of their forefathers.

Over the years kings and rulers came and went, but the Jews remained. Persia replaced Parthia, Sasanian princes overthrew the nobles of the Arsacid throne, but the Jews multiplied and flourished, creating a major center into which the goods of the entire world flowed. During a few heady years Nehardea even became an independent Jewish realm ruled by two Jewish brothers - weavers by trade - who not only rebelled against their master-weaver, but against imperial Rome itself. The end of this independent Jewish realm - like the end of all things mortal - had come soon enough. But no matter what tempestuous winds of history were blowing, Nehardea continued to thrive, and even after the destruction by Odenathus - may his name be blotted out - a mere dozen years earlier, it soon rose out of the ashes to achieve even greater glory.

* * *

This morning the streets of Nehardea lay quiet, still slumbering peacefully in the final moments before dawn. At this early hour of the morning only the Arab shepherds would be up and abroad, guiding flocks of sheep and goats down to the pastures outside the city's ancient walls. The very houses themselves appeared fast asleep, their slumbers guarded by high, whitewashed walls and those dozing sentries, the date-palms. But behind closed doors, the town was wide awake, astir with gossip of the liveliest kind. Everyone knew that Samuel's daughter had just come back - Rachel - the little girl born just after her father's death and taken captive at the fall of Nehardea when she was only four years old. Here and there housewives pattered out to the door and craned their necks in the direction of Chana's house, hoping for a glimpse of the newly returned captive. Even the men, reciting their morning prayers, could not refrain from letting their thoughts wander over to the widow's house, where the captive was probably now asleep. Samuel's little daughter. Well, well, well. Praised be He who brings back the dead.

The birds began chirping, the sun rose from behind the morning clouds, and it suddenly seemed to the good housewives of Nehardea that it might be a very good idea if they went to the well and drew their own water that morning. Let the serving girls have a rest for once. Even the women who were not obliged to do anything more strenuous for their households than work in wool, or ply their needle, were feeling unusually benevolent today. So armed with these virtuous intentions, and with whatever pitcher came to hand, the women made their way to the well, not too surprised to discover that their neighbors had all had the same good idea. Even the younger girls, dutifully following their mothers, went forth in the chill, clear dawn of a winter's morning, straining their ears to hear what they could.

No need, of course, to explain who Samuel was! Even the youngest girls, born after Samuel's death some fifteen years earlier, or even after the subsequent invasion of Nehardea, knew that Samuel had been one of the two great judges of Babylonian Jewry. Samuel and Rav - these were the two most revered names in the Jewish communities that dotted the fertile region between the Tigris and the Euphrates. These were the names people quoted when they went to the rabbis with their disputes over leases, or inheritance, or divorce. In Nehardea, however, it was Samuel who ruled supreme, and as far as the Nehardean *qab* extended, so too did Samuel's jurisdiction. There was a saying that anyone who did not know Samuel's judgments knew nothing about civil law, and years after his death people still quoted his sayings and cited his rulings. Even Rabbi Nachman, who now presided over the Court, treated Samuel's decisions with reverence and respect. Or at least - some people whispered - when it was convenient for him to do so.

People also recalled the friendship between Samuel and Shapur, the great King of Persia who held Nehardea and all Babylonia in sway. Remember the time - they would fondly reminisce - that Shapur invited Samuel to partake of the new fruits with him? Why, he stuck his knife in the earth eight times out of respect for Samuel and his observance of the Law. Or the time that Samuel juggled eight bottles of wines before the King? And on one occasion, Shapur had even deigned to discuss the coming of the Messiah with Samuel, and upon learning that the Messiah was due to arrive on a white donkey, offered to send a white Persian steed in its place. "Ah," Samuel had replied, "haven't you a hundred-colored horse to send instead?" What a card, that Samuel! What a diplomat!

All this and more, everyone in Nehardea knew. But what many of the younger girls at the well that morning did not know, was the subsequent fate of Samuel's family. There had been three daughters, all that was left to Samuel and his wife after the death of their sons. Now the youngest girls learned for the first time that Samuel's two oldest daughters had been taken captive in the destruction of Nehardea by Odenathus - may his name be blotted out - and ransomed soon after by the Jewish community in the Land of Israel, after being taken there by pirates. But the youngest girl, Rachel, had disappeared without a trace, snatched no doubt from the very arms of her mother, whose body had been found amidst the wreckage of their beautiful mansion. And now, this very Rachel had come back after years of captivity amongst the uncivilized tribes of far-away Parthia.

The girls sighed. For them, all this was as good as a Greek romance, the kind they heard in the market place when they had a chance to escape the watchful eyes of their nurses. Greek romances always had pirates, and no doubt Rachel would be pale and interesting. Though of course totally barbaric. They would have to teach the poor girl - kindly of course! - how to be a good Jewish daughter. They would have to show her how to say her prayers, and how to prepare food as behooved a pious Jewish maiden. In fact, they could hardly wait to begin their pious duty - if only they could just go to Chana's house and knock on the door! But Chana might not be pleased by that, and it was best to wait for the girl to appear on her own.

The mothers, for their part, were thinking of matters of an even more immediate nature. Let's see now . . . the girl must be seventeen, eighteen years old now, a ripe fig indeed. But was her sweetness intact? The mothers huddled together over this one, shaking their heads in doubt and anxiety. Who knew what the rabbis would decide? And, hadn't Samuel betrothed Rachel to Rabbi Huna's son, even before Rachel was born? What would Chana say to that? Or Rabbi Huna himself? And most important - what would Yalta, Rabbi Nachman's wife, have to say? Ahhh, that was the question. The women shook their head in pity. Rachel would not have an easy time of it.

News of the captive's return continued to fly through the town, whispering into the ears of morning shoppers and slipping into the dreams of those still asleep. It even made its way into the courtroom of Rabbi Nachman, though here it had had to cool its heels a bit in the ante-room, for it was a busy morning in court. Rabbi Nachman had entered the courtroom as usual that morning, and, with a dignified nod at the students standing in front of him, settled down to hear his first case, when a woman burst in, crying at the top of her lungs. "They're feasting under a stolen pergola!" she screamed. Rabbi Nachman frowned at the interruption, but the woman was not to be stopped by such trivia. "I demand justice!" she screamed again, and stamped her foot for emphasis.

"Let the first defendant make his case," Rabbi Nachman replied, motioning to his servants to throw the woman out. But this only increased her fury.

"The Exilarch's servants stole the wood for their pergola from my yard," she informed the room at large. "They took the planks from under my very nose!" Rabbi Nachman again motioned to his servants, but the woman shook them off angrily. "Why don't you listen to my cries?" she demanded, facing Rabbi Nachman. "You and your paltry servants. Bah! Who do you think you are? Me, I'm the daughter of Father Abraham, and in my house we had three-hundred-and-eighteen servants. Three-hundred-and-eighteen! Though no one pays any attention to me *here*," she added huffily.

Row after row, the students shifted nervously. "Imagine coming here with complaints about the Exilarch," they whispered to each other. But Rabbi Nachman paid no heed. "She's a noisy woman," he remarked, making a ruling with a quick motion of his hand. "All she gets is the money for the wood!" With that, his servants finally managed to push the woman out of the room, still screaming about the stolen pergola and her planks of wood.

Rabbi Nachman, son of Jacob, was the son-in-law of the Exilarch, Rabbah bar Avuha. As the acknowledged scion of the House of David, ancient king of Israel, the Exilarch represented the Jews before the Persian authorities, and Rabbi Nachman had the name of his mighty father-in-law on his lips six times a day. "Otherwise," he would ask himself reasonably, "what was the point of being married to Yalta?" So in the name of the Exilarch, Rabbi Nachman lorded it over the Jews of Nehardea, and anyone else who had the misfortune to run afoul of his pride. People still recalled the time he had Rabbi Judah bar Ezekiel hauled into court over some trifling incident in a butcher shop - and Rabbi Judah the Head of the Academy in Pumbedita! Safe in the protection of the Exilarch, Rabbi Nachman was quick to overturn any decision that did not suit him. Once he even declared that were he to hear a contrary decision from the lips of Samuel himself, may he rest in peace, he would still refuse to change his mind.

His wealth was proverbial. When Rabbi Nachman set out in his golden litter, dressed in purple-dyed wool like royalty, his servants ran in front of him brandishing whips and rods, ready to beat anyone who failed to pay proper respect to their master or to submit to his judgment. People might grumble and complain - in fact they frequently did - but as Rabbi Nachman would tranquilly remind them, "I am the judge - and you are not."

Rabbi Nachman had not reached his high position without hard work and study. "Where would I be without all my learning?" he liked to say modestly. "Without it, there are lots of Nachmans in the market-place!" It was this learning that had brought him to the attention of the illustrious Rabbah bar Avuha, Exilarch of Babylonia. A precocious child, Nachman had been taken by his father - a judge in Samuel's court - to attend the Exilarch's school. There, the Exilarch was so impressed with the boy's perspicacity that he betrothed him to his own daughter, Yalta - a doubtful prize in the opinion of some. Rumor had it that even Rabbi Nachman was afraid of his wife's sharp tongue, and certainly she was the terror of many a local housewife. But with the backing of his powerful father-in-law, Nachman had been able to institute far-reaching changes in the court that had once been Samuel's. In Samuel's day all cases had been heard by three judges, but now that Rabbi Nachman presided over the court, all that had changed and now it was a rare case indeed that had the benefit of any judge apart from himself.

So, installed in his solitary glory, Rabbi Nachman settled himself into his seat to resume business as usual. Yet, no sooner had the defendants for the first case taken their stand than the sound of a woman's voice out in the corridor again interrupted the proceedings. "That pesky woman!" Rabbi Nachman said, showing his irritation at last. "Take her by the ear and throw her . . ." But where his servants were to throw her the courtroom was never privileged to learn. The woman burst into the room, and Rabbi Nachman turned pale. "Yalta!" he said, considerably flustered. He jumped to his feet.

Yalta, the wife of Rabbi Nachman, was the daughter of the Exilarch - and she never let anyone forget it, her husband least of all. The rules governing feminine modesty were fine for other women, but Yalta was a law unto herself. People still enjoying relating what happened the time that Rabbi Ulla, a renowned scholar visiting from the Land of Israel, declined to drink to Yalta's health one Sabbath eve, though the toast was proposed by Nachman himself. Now, this was an honor that Ulla refused any woman; but no matter: Yalta took the refusal as a personal insult and responded as any woman of spirit was bound to respond, namely, by smashing four barrels of wine - and there were those who swore that it was actually four hundred. Whatever the number, Yalta certainly made her point, and after that only the rash, or the brave, failed to walk gingerly where Yalta was concerned.

"Nachman!" she now said imperiously. "You must come home. We have things to discuss."

"Yes, dear, of course," Rabbi Nachman said nervously, glaring at his students to see if there was even a trace of a smile on anyone's lips. There wasn't, of course. Who would dare to smile with Yalta in the room? So Rabbi Nachman dismissed the proceedings till the next day and followed his wife obediently out of the courtroom.

The beautiful villa in which Nachman and Yalta dwelled was only a few steps from the court-house, so ignoring the bearers of his sedan-chair and followed only by Daro, his ever-faithful servant, he and Yalta walked home in a dignified silence. But once there, Yalta did not keep her husband in suspense. "You'll never guess what's happened!" she said.

"What - " Rabbi Nachman tried to ask."Don't interrupt!" Yalta ordered. "Guess who is back in Nehardea."

"Who - " he tried again, before Yalta stopped him. "If you'll be quiet a moment," she said, exasperated, "I'll tell you." She paused for greater effect. "It's Rachel, Samuel's daughter, the one who disappeared during the burning of Nehardea twelve years ago."

Rabbi Nachman did not even repeat the words of blessing customary upon the return of a captive. Like Yalta, he immediately understood the implications this might have for his own family and his agile mind leaped into action. "Where is Doneg?" he inquired, referring to his eldest daughter.

"Out at the well," Yalta told him. "She's there with all the other girls, talking about Rachel as though the Messiah himself had come to town."

Rabbi Nachman considered the situation. Doneg was betrothed to Rabbi Huna's son, Rami. He and Huna had arranged the match long ago. Before that, it is true, Rami had been destined for Rachel, but he and Rachel had never been formally betrothed, for Samuel, may he rest in peace, had died before Rachel was even born, and Rachel herself had been considered as good as dead these last fifteen years or so. The betrothal between Rami and Doneg, on the other hand, had been as formal as the letter of the law could make it, and their marriage was due to take place next winter, Rabbi Huna being firmly of the opinion that no man, and certainly no son of his, should remain single beyond the age of twenty. To break the engagement between Doneg and Rami at this point would require nothing less than a formal bill of divorce for his daughter, for such was the law in these cases, and no amount of legal casuistry could get around that sad fact.

As all this was going through his head, Rabbi Nachman started feeling rather sorry for himself, and indeed somewhat aggrieved. Under different circumstances he could have rejoiced most sincerely at the return of Samuel's daughter from captivity, but this situation involved his own daughter, and under no circumstance would he allow Doneg to be so disgraced. In fact, it would disgrace the whole family if Rabbi Huna decided to break off the engagement, no matter how compelling the circumstances might be. Rabbi Nachman sighed and felt more aggrieved than ever. Was it his fault that Rachel had chosen this moment to return? He sighed again and looked around the large atrium in which he and Yalta were sitting, noting with heightened awareness the elegance of its proportions and the grandeur of its fittings. His family disgraced? The very idea made him shudder.

He spoke up firmly. "Well, what if Rachel has come back? Should things be any different just because a captive has returned? She may be Samuel's daughter, but Samuel, may he rest in peace, is dead, and Doneg is the daughter of the Chief Judge of Nehardea. And," he continued hastily, noting Yalta's displeasure, "the daughter of the Exilarch's own daughter." Yalta nodded, appeased. "Why then," Rabbi Nachman continued," would Rabbi Huna want to marry his son to anyone else?"

"Yes, but . . ." Yalta broke in.

"No buts about it," her husband replied at his lordliest - something Yalta rarely permitted. "Rachel hadn't even been born when Samuel betrothed her to Huna's son - and Rami himself was just a child. When the time comes, I'll know just what to do." He gave Yalta a sly smile. "In fact, he added cryptically, "I'll deal with this just as Samuel himself would have done. No one will be able to complain." And with that Yalta had to be content.

* * *

Midmorning drew on, and still no sign of the captive. Pazi, Rabbi Menachem's wife, took courage in both hands and went up to Chana's house. Surely a neighbor could borrow a bit of flour? She knocked on the door. After a while she heard footsteps coming down the corridor and her heart gave a flutter, but to her great disappointment the door was opened by Tavi, Chana's housekeeper, who listened to Pazi's stammered request with a look of patent disbelief and bade her remain outside. A few minutes later Chana herself appeared, a middle-aged woman, comely and rounded, with dark hair only faintly touched with grey and gathered into a knot at the nape of her neck. As the widow of Samuel's brother, Phineas, she was Rachel's aunt both by blood and by marriage; her sister, Shulamit, had been Samuel's wife and the mother of all his children. Chana looked like the intelligent woman she was, and her bearing was dignified and quiet; sometimes, perhaps, to the point of rather intimidating the weaker spirits around her. Nevertheless, anyone who looked closely would have seen that her eyes were not without humor, and that her glance betrayed a certain wry insight into the frailties of human nature in general, and of her neighbors in particular. Chana stepped outside to greet Pazi, whom she had known all her life.

"Good morning, Pazi. Peace be upon you."

"And peace upon you, Chana. I've just come to borrow some flour," Pazi explained with a nonchalant air. "The barges didn't arrive yesterday, and I find myself a bit short."

"Oh!" said Chana with a surprised look, "I thought perhaps you might want to see Rachel."

Pazi tried to look offended, and failed. She smiled sheepishly at Chana and said, "Well, yes, as a matter of fact, I *would* like a glimpse. As you know, her mother, may she rest in peace, was one of my best friends – indeed we practically grew up together."

Chana smiled. "Of course. But Rachel's been traveling, as you know, and she needs her rest today. And time to get used to everything. Perhaps next week . . ."

Pazi's face fell. There would be no glimpse of Rachel that morning.

Chana closed the door behind her with a glint of amusement in her eyes, and returning down the corridor she crossed the courtyard and went back into the kitchen where she had been sitting with her brother Eliezer, whom the good Jews of Nehardea nicknamed Rabbi Strabo on account of his endless maps and scrolls about far-away places. Like Chana, Eliezer had been widowed for many years now, and though he had his own house in Nehardea he was often to be found visiting his sister for he had no surviving children, and Chana's two sons were both of them grown and living far away in the great trading centers along the coast of Syria. It was still early morning, and the two sat companionably over their bread and olives, basking in the warm winter sunshine flooding the courtyard, for the kitchen opened wide onto its columned expanse. Tavi was busy at the oven, twisting loaves of dough in preparation for the Sabbath.

"So, what's she like, Chana?" Rabbi Strabo asked with a smile. "It's to be hoped that she doesn't take after her father, may he rest in peace, what with those teeth of his and that big stomach, and . . ."

"Now, Eliezer," Chana rebuked him, repressing a smile. "That's no way to talk about a great scholar like Samuel. And you know what they say: 'don't look at a girl's beauty; look at her family's lineage'."

Rabbi Strabo laughed, and took another olive. "Yes, that's what they say. But then I'm not looking to marry her! So, what *doe*s she look like?"

"Look like?" Tavi snorted from her place by the oven. "She looks like any of those heathen fire-worshippers. What did you expect?"

Since those "heathen fire-worshippers," as Tavi put it, looked remarkably like the rest of the local population, Jew and gentile alike, Chana tactfully ignored Tavi's comment. "Well," she said thoughtfully, "she looks like her mother, more so than either of her sisters. And she's just as pretty as Shulamit was. Her hair is long and rather wavy, and she definitely has Shulamit's eyes - remember, Eliezer? - very deep and dark, with that look about them as though she were always dreaming. And those same black lashes. She's not quite as fair-skinned as her sisters, but no doubt that's because of the way she lived back in Parthia. Her captors probably had her working out in the fields all day long."

"Not her!" Tavi contradicted her mistress, breaking into the conversation again. "Not at the hours she keeps! Why, she's still in bed sleeping."

"Please wake her up, then," Chana instructed, "so she can meet her uncle." Tavi went off, grumbling, and Rabbi Strabo laughed outright.

"I take it Tavi doesn't approve of Rachel," he said comfortably, "but then, she doesn't approve of me either. What's she done to irk her?"

Chana ignored the question, and instead just remarked, "Well, you can hardly expect Tavi to approve of you, pagan that you are. You and your scrolls about far-away heathen places. Now if you were a scholar like Samuel, may he rest in peace . . . "

"Samuel!" Rabbi Strabo said indignantly, pushing away the olives. "Some scholar. Why, he didn't even know where Harev is. Once I told him that the Silk Road to Bactria led through Harev, and he said, 'Wasn't that where Moses saw the burning bush?'"

"Samuel was a great scholar," Chana said firmly, "and everyone knows it. Why even the King respected him! And the King's mother too, may she rest in peace. How else do you think that Samuel managed to betroth Rachel to Rabbi Huna's son? Why, she hadn't even been born, and Huna, rich man that he is, jumped at the chance to marry her to his son."

"Yes, what about that betrothal?" Rabbi Strabo asked curiously, though still not reconciled to the fact that Samuel had not been able to put the great city of Harev on the map. "What will happen now? It seems to me that Huna went and betrothed that son of his to Rabbi Nachman's daughter, what's-her-name. Or have I heard wrong?"

Chana paused a few moments before answering. "No," she said slowly, "you haven't heard wrong. Huna did betroth his son to Doneg. But now he'll just have to un-betroth her and make other arrangements. Rachel has come back, and I'm determined to see that she marry Huna's son, just as her father intended, and that she resume her rightful place here in Babylonia as Samuel's daughter."

"But Chana," Rabbi Strabo answered, rather startled, "Doneg is Rabbi Nachman's daughter. And even worse," he added impressively, "she's *Yalta's* daughter. You know what Yalta's like, and Nachman himself will not be so accommodating, you know, and furthermore . . ."

In the meantime, the source of all the commotion was wide awake, resting under a warm woolen blanket in the upper story of her aunt's house, listening to the calls of the shepherds and to the noise of the little boys on their way to school. On this, her first morning in Nehardea, Rachel found herself fascinated by the unfamiliar sounds of town life that wafted into her room through the open window. Every now and then a wagon rumbled down the cobbled streets, and neighbors wished each other good morning on the way to synagogue or the market-place. She lay in bed just soaking in these first impressions, unable to believe that she was here, actually here in this place called Babylonia so far away from her home across the great mountains. She, Rachel, the daughter of Kovad - she had not yet begun to think of herself as having any other name.

Her thoughts went back to the night it all began: that night during the feast of *Mihragan*, when those two strangers with the foreign accent had wandered into their festivities around the fire-altar and engaged the girls there in talk. She had been surprised, indeed startled, by the curious interest which they evinced in herself and her name, but she had not thought the incident of any special consequence, and indeed the strangers had soon gone their way in search of their caravan. The only immediate consequence of that evening, in fact, had been a sorely offended sister, grieved to think that Rachel had been keeping secrets from her all these years. After all, Rachel had never said anything to *her* about this Samuel!

"But I haven't been keeping secrets," Rachel protested again and again, hot in self-defense and anxious to appease her sister. "I honestly don't know how it happened. I think it was something in the way they spoke, or the way they said my name . . ." And it was true. Rachel herself didn't understand how the name "Samuel" suddenly rose to her lips. Where had it come from, this name; where had it been hiding all these years? But the moment she spoke she knew she'd spoken truly, and for just a moment she'd had a memory of another world; a spacious world of white-columned rooms and sunlit gardens, of roses and trees and the sound of splashing water. Of women who dressed her and combed out her hair, who played with her by the hour and called her by name. But just for a split second. Then the memory went dark, and again she was in Parthia with her sister Shirin and the villagers she had known all her life, and again she saw the leaping flames of the fire altar casting mysterious shadows in the forest around them. She had not been able to remember anything else, and the more the strangers prodded, the more silent she became. It was as though a deep forest, cavernous and black, had been illuminated for the briefest moment by a flash of lightening, and then reverted to darkness.

It was several days before Shirin forgave her sister, though Rachel did not quite understand what she had done wrong, or just why she needed forgiving. Indeed, Shirin was hard put to understand her feelings herself. Was she upset because Rachel had been keeping secrets from her? Or because Rachel was . . . was . . .? Shirin couldn't say. So after a while she forgave Rachel and the two girls never referred to that evening again. But in some indefinable way, something had changed. Indeed everything changed. After that night Shirin spent more and more time with her friends, and she no longer included Rachel in all their activities or bossed her around in the big-sisterly way she had always done up until now. Why this should be so, Shirin couldn't say. It was all done without forethought - she only knew that something had changed.

Rachel also felt the difference, but she was too absorbed by the changes taking place in her own self to be fully cognizant of the growing breach with her family, or as grieved over it as she would have been in former times. In some subtle way, Rachel felt as though the very core of her being was shifting; turning away from the world she had known until now and realigning itself with that one single moment; the moment when the strangers had asked their question and the forest had dissolved into memory. That house, the gardens, the women . . . again and again she strained after the image that had flashed upon her so unawares, but without success; all she had now was the memory of a memory. But she yearned for the memory of that place nevertheless, telling herself without words: There. *There*. That was where she had been meant to be.

Even Mother, who had not been present that night and had only heard of the meeting second-hand from a distraught Shirin, became more and more thoughtful as time went by. And all of a sudden she found her thoughts straying back to an incident that had occurred long ago, indeed not long after Rachel first appeared in the Gurgan Valley, perched on the saddlebags of Kovad's horse. It had been years since she'd thought about that incident, yet now the memory of it came flooding back to her as clearly as though it had happened only yesterday:

It was early springtime, she recalled, and Kovad had just returned from the wars with this little girl in tow. One morning, soon after his return, Kovad decided to ask the local priest for his blessing over the child, so placing Rachel before him on the saddle, he and Vis rode down the mountain-sides to seek the priest out. As their horses picked their way nimbly down the craggy slopes, Vis could feel the air becoming mistier, shrouding the green tops of the vast beech forest into which they were riding. They found the holy man at his work in the rough wooden hut adjoining the fire-altar, and Kovad, who had been carrying the little girl in his arms, set her down on the floor. The priest duly gave the child his blessing, and then, being a convivial fellow and fond of company, fell into conversation with Kovad, so newly back from the great world beyond the mountains. Vis listened on, enjoying the lively conversation and contributing an occasional word or two. Thus engrossed in Kovad's description of the rich lands beyond their valley, the three adults were startled to hear Rachel suddenly pipe out, and in a most cheerful voice: "I can read, too!" and turning around, saw that the child had climbed up a chair and was kneeling, elbows on table, over a broad work-surface covered with scrolls. This was unexpected, to say the least! The convivial priest, suddenly on his guard, muttered a charm against demons: you never knew. Vis and Kovad stared dumbfounded: never before had they met a child who could read. In fact, they had never met *anyone* who could read, apart from this village priest. And so it was with a great deal of unease, and more than a little anxiety, that they all watched the child getting ready to show off her talents. She unrolled a scroll as though searching for a particular place, stopped at the chosen text and smoothed it out, and then running her fore-finger underneath the words, began to read them out loud. They listened, thunderstruck, when all of a sudden Vis began to laugh. She laughed so hard she nearly cried, greatly amused - and more than a little relieved.

"She's not reading!" she said. "She's repeating the story I told her and Shirin last night, before going to sleep!"

Kovad burst into laughter, in which the priest heartily joined in (though not before mumbling another quick charm), and Vis promptly lifted Rachel off the chair and set her back down on the ground, before she could make any more mischief. And that was the end of the matter. Rachel was no more able to read than Shirin or Issur or anyone else in the valley. But Vis had noticed the way the little girl smoothed the scroll out with her fingers, the expert way she unrolled the length of parchment, and the care with which she had rolled it back up again. And in her heart Vis thought, "She comes from a line of scholars, or priests," and was gripped by a sudden fear. Was this child really for them?

Almost a year went by after that meeting with the two strangers in the mountains. The weeks mellowed into fall and then froze into winter. Again the mountain pastures were covered with the rich swards of spring, and again at summer's end the cowherds brought the cattle back down the mountains amidst the songs and festivities of the village children. Then one day towards *Mihragan* and the first golden leaves of autumn, strangers again appeared in the valley. Only, this time it was not by accident or because they were separated from their caravan. These men were actually looking for Rachel, asking for the girl by name.

Rachel and Shirin had been standing in the kitchen, cooking dinner over the blazing hearth when they heard men with strange voices talking first with the cowherd out by the granary, and then with Mother on her way back from the barn. Something in the strangers' voices, in the way they pronounced certain words, distinctly recalled the conversation with the merchants that night, and as Shirin looked up in surprise Rachel turned white and stuck her elbow into the burning cauldron, as though to test the temperature.

The two strangers paused at the threshold, a look of dismay on their faces as they took in the scene. "So that's Samuel's daughter!" one of them said, immediately fixing his gaze on Rachel. "They've made a real *bondag* out of her."

"What barbarian ways she has learned," said the other, distastefully.

The merchants hadn't had an easy time of it. They had come to ransom Rachel from captivity, and this they proceeded to do in due form. One of the men pulled out a leathern pouch and set it down on the table with a significant ringing of coins; the other took a letter from beneath the folds of his tunic and unrolled it before the gaping crowd, for word of these strange events had flown through the valley and from near and far the neighbors had gathered to listen. Even the cowherds were seen loitering around the front door. The stranger read the letter before a hushed audience:

> *To the nobles and princes that art in Babylonia, remnants of the dispersed tribes of Israel, greetings from the holy community of Nehardea. We turn to you on behalf of a captive who stands in need of your assistance. Know that we are speaking of the daughter of the great Rabbi Samuel, may he rest in peace, taken captive during the depredations of Odenathus, may his seed be blotted out, and given up for dead. But God is great, and she, the*

said captive, has now been found in the wilds of Parthia where she awaits the ransom that will restore her to freedom and family. We, the holy community of Nehardea, have raised the sum of thirty-three golden dinars which we do entrust into the hands of reliable brethren, merchants familiar with the routes through the mountain passes, and ask that all possible assistance . . .

The stranger read on to the end of the letter, and then, perfectly aware that none of these locals had understood a word he said, he acquainted them with the facts in the language they knew. Again there was a hushed silence. And when he finished, Mother stepped forward.

"But Rachel isn't a captive," she said quietly, "and there is no need for ransom. Return the coins to your bosom, O stranger."

The merchants had not had an easy time of it. Had Father still been alive, Rachel knew that she would still be in the valley, probably married to Issur and with a farmhouse of her own, but Father had died last winter and Issur was away at the wars with the other young men. She completely forgot that she had ever dreamed of other places, ever imagined another life for herself. She regretted - fiercely regretted - that she had ever answered those strangers or opened her mouth before them.

It came as no little shock, therefore, when she saw that Mother was not only ready to let her go with these strangers but indeed appeared, in some curious way, almost to have expected this moment. Rachel turned to Shirin with a mute gesture of appeal, but Shirin too seemed curiously resigned to the idea of Rachel's departure. Such stoicism on the part of her volatile sister surprised Rachel - surprised and deeply hurt her. But only for a moment. Then the memory of that fateful night flashed again through her brain, and she stood silently, head bowed, unable to speak and scarcely able to think.

Everything now moved quickly. The merchants were anxious to continue their journey and seemed impatient at the delay. They looked significantly at the lengthening shadows outside, and in the end they took Rachel with them. Mother parted with Rachel on the threshold of their home, blessing her with the ancient words bestowed on all pious travelers, but Shirin rode with Rachel part of the way down the mountain, in and out of the great beech forest with its dim shadows and golden shafts of light, riding in silence till they reached the wooded slope where a camel caravan stood waiting. She and Rachel dismounted, and watched as the servants took Rachel's bundles, strapping them onto the camel they had brought for Samuel's daughter. Somehow it was the sight of that camel that suddenly made the whole situation real for Rachel. For although she had often seen camels crossing the valley in caravans on their way to the east, or tethered together at the market-place during the annual fair at *Nauruz*, she had never seen one so close, and it was with sudden fear that Rachel turned to her sister.

"It'll be just for a while," Rachel told Shirin nervously, and at that moment she believed what she said. "Just for a year, or two at the most. Then I'll find a way to come back, I promise."

"You'd better," Shirin replied, with an attempt at lightness, gathering up the reigns to Rachel's horse and preparing to go back up the mountain. Her face was hidden, for she was watching the horses drink from the stream, and Rachel could not quite see her expression. But then looking up, she said with a voice that was unexpectedly grim, "If not, you can bet that Issur will come and get you."

A sudden noise outside her room put an end to Rachel's reveries and brought her back to the present. With a perfunctory knock at the door, Tavi stuck her head in the room and said sourly: "Your aunt wants you." Disapproval was writ large on her face.

Rousing herself from her thoughts, Rachel rose, washed her face and hands in the basin that Tavi set down for her, and pinning the folds of her *chiton* to her left shoulder, as Tavi told her she should, she descended the stairs into the courtyard. Unused to dress that hampered her feet she took care not to trip on the steps, wondering all the while just how she was supposed to ride a horse in such clothing.

Rabbi Strabo looked up with interest as Rachel came into the room, pushing his chair back from the table. Like many of the men she had seen since leaving Parthia, her uncle had short hair and a closely-cut beard, and he was dressed in a white linen robe not too different from the one she was wearing herself, though his had a different kind of design near the hem and left some of the leg bare above the ankle. He greeted her with acclaim.

"Welcome to Nehardea! Welcome back, I should say. I hear they found you in the Gurgan district," he added, unfurling his maps and spreading them across the table. "The Gurgan district," he said, for the benefit of his sister, "is of course the classical Hyrcania, and the Vehrkano of the *Avesta*. Strabo says that in Hyrcania each vine produces seven gallons of wine and that each fig tree yields ninety bushels of fruit. That the grains of wheat which fall from the husk onto the earth spring up the following year; that there are beehives in the trees and that the leaves flow with honey." He paused and looked expectantly up at the girl.

"It is a very fertile country," she agreed, somewhat startled.

"How was your trip across the mountain passes? You'll have to tell me all about it. Did you pass through Rhagae and the Caspian Gates? Alexander himself went through that route, you know. Or did you take the alternate route through . . ."

Chana interrupted, not knowing whether to laugh or be angry. "Eliezer, be quiet!" she ordered. "Rachel's just back, and she has more to do than make a geographer's report to you. Rachel, come kiss your uncle."

Rachel came forward as bidden and bent low to kiss the old man's hand. He was plump and cheerful, with a great booming voice, and she liked him at first sight. "We saw tigers and hyenas, and passed underneath a picture of the King of Kings carved into the mountain sides," she whispered into his ear. Rabbi Strabo looked at the girl with an approving smile.

"The Caspian Gates?" asked Tavi with interest, forgetting for a moment her character of heathen-hater. "Are they made of pure gold, like they say? And covered with rubies and diamonds and -" But Rachel shook her head. "They're not gates at all," she explained. "Just a kind of road carved through high mountains on either side." At which Tavi just looked disgusted and shook her head, like one who should have known better than to expect anything much from heathens. Chana cleared her throat to regain their attention, at which they all lifted inquiring eyes.

"Rachel," she said firmly, "you must sit *shiva* for your mother. Now that you are back, you must mourn your mother for the full week of mourning."

Chapter Seven

The week of mourning passed slowly, but once it came to an end Rachel began to enjoy her stay in Nehardea and to take pleasure in the amenities of town life. Every day was market-day here. Nehardea was a hub of international trade and the goods of the world flowed into its busy shops. The local girls came to call on her, and looked at her with interest. She looked back at them, no less curious than they, though considerably less voluble. They wore graceful robes of white linen edged with purple or blue, and silver bangles from the markets of Media and Elymais. They asked her questions and laughed at her accent, and her ignorance, and in between prayers at synagogue talked importantly about their upcoming marriages and pointed out their bridegrooms-to-be.

Rachel's first order of business, naturally enough, was to learn about her family and to check her own memories, few as they were, with such facts as Chana and Eliezer could tell her. She told them about the memory that had flashed upon her so suddenly in the forest that fateful night, and Chana and Eliezer both nodded their heads in corroboration: yes, the paternal mansion in which she had lived those few short years in Nehardea had been white and spacious, with a high-columned atrium overlooking rose gardens and carob trees, and the women she remembered must have been her mother and sisters, or perhaps the maid-servants, of which there had been not a few. Rachel then said, somewhat more diffidently, and as though as an after-thought, that she thought she could remember having climbed (and also fallen out of) a lot of trees, torn her clothes in any number of rose bushes, and run freely through the house and gardens. In short, a veritable household terror - wasn't that so, she asked earnestly? But on this point her aunt and uncle were unable to enlighten her. During most of Rachel's childhood Chana had lived in the great trading center of Antioch-on-the-Orontes, busy with her husband and sons and the cares of a large household, and during that time had only seen Rachel once, when Rachel was but an infant. And as for letters from Rachel's mother, Shulamit - Chana waved a dismissive hand. "But I do remember your mother bragging that you were a quiet child, and almost never made any noise," she added, beaming, as though this could compensate for never having seen Rachel fall out of a carob tree. Rachel's heart fell. And her uncle, it turned out, had also been away from Nehardea during those same years, living up river in the city of Pumbedita, where he had cultivated flax and run a thriving linen-weaving business. It was only after Chana's bereavement and subsequent removal to Nehardea, two years after the destruction by Odenathus, that Eliezer himself returned to the city of his birth. Letters from Shulamit? He shook his head: the only thing he could remember reading during those years, apart from the Torah, of course, and his letters of business, was his precious scroll of Strabo; it was in Pumbedita, he informed Rachel triumphantly, that he had first acquired that scroll. Thus neither Chana nor Eliezer could throw much light on the questions that so absorbed Rachel, and she put her hopes on the letters that must soon come from her sisters in the Land of Israel - surely they would tell her everything she wished to know.

In any event, Chana was a woman with a strong practical bent, less interested in recalling the glories of the past than in dealing with the exigencies of the present. And *her* first order of business was to turn her niece into the pious Jewish maiden that a daughter of Samuel ought to be. Hence she launched her instructions almost immediately, teaching Rachel the basic prayers for home and for synagogue, the laws concerning the preparation of food, and the laws concerning ritual immersion and hygiene. Only, Rachel, alas, did not always take kindly to instruction. It was not, Chana thought, that Rachel was disobedient or headstrong, God forbid, but rather that she never really seemed to take seriously anything that she, Chana, tried to teach her. How many times had she had to tell Rachel not to begin her meal before saying the benediction?

"Your father," she'd had to say severely on more than one occasion, "used to say that to enjoy anything of this world without saying the benediction was like making personal use of things consecrated to Heaven. For is it not written, that *the earth is the Lord's and the fullness thereof*?"

As far as Chana was concerned, these lessons were a mild enough beginning for a young girl with so much to learn, but what she didn't quite realize - perhaps couldn't realize, because her world had always been Jewish - was how strange this new world felt to Rachel, and how different it all seemed to her. Everything there aroused Rachel's wonder: the whitewashed houses and the towering date-palms; the thronging market place that always magically reappeared the next morning, rather than next year; even the unchanging blue of the skies, where clouds were almost never to be seen after the first morning haze. The synagogue, around which so much of her new life revolved, aroused her wonder by the very fact of its existence.

"Oh, yes," Chana had replied, pleased, when Rachel had expressed her wonder over this building. "It *is* very beautiful, isn't it? And it has some remarkable features; I hear, for example, that this is the only synagogue in the world with a statue in it; Rabbi Jonathan says so, and he's traveled *everywhere.* Been up and down Arabia I don't know how many times. And then there's the Torah shrine, which has -"

But Rachel interrupted her aunt at this point, shaking her head. "It *is* beautiful," she said, "but that's not what I meant. I mean, that the very idea of having a special building to pray in seems strange to me. For back in Parthia, you see, we said our prayers at home, before the fire, and there was no central place, or certainly no building, for saying them."

"No?" Chana asked absently, not terribly interested in heathen prayer rites.

"No," Rachel confirmed; and then, without knowing it, recaptured her aunt's attention by asking a most amazing question. "What makes it holy for praying?" she inquired.

Chana was dumbfounded by the question, and for a moment almost suspected Rachel of impertinence. What made the synagogue holy? "Why, it just is!" was what she wanted to say, and in fact almost did. But then she realized that Rachel had asked the question in all innocence, and that this was as good a time as any for giving her niece an impromptu lesson in Judaism. So she coughed a bit.

"Well," she said, "the sages tell us that when the Temple in Jerusalem was destroyed and the Jews sent into Exile, God Himself was grieved. And just as a gazelle skips from thicket to thicket and from grove to grove, so does He leap from synagogue to synagogue, to be with them." She bit back the words "in their forest of exile," as being too dramatic for the occasion.

"Oh," said Rachel, registering this thoughtfully. "Then you mean, that every synagogue is holy, and not just this one."

"Well, yes," Chana acknowledged, a shade reluctantly, not liking to admit that other synagogues might have a claim to sanctity. "Though of course this one is holier than any of the others," and she forestalled the question she saw on Rachel's lips by saying, "Ask your uncle."

Later that night Rachel did ask her uncle and Rabbi Strabo told her about the foundation stones brought from the Temple by the exiles of Judea. "And just to give you an idea of how holy this synagogue is," he added, "people say that when Abba ben Abba - that's your grandfather, you know - studied there together with his friend Levi ben Sisi, the Divine Presence would actually hover over them."

"It did?" Rachel asked, impressed.

Rabbi Strabo nodded solemnly, and then ruined it all by adding, with a decided twinkle in his eye, "Though Chana probably didn't tell you that it was probably due as much to Levi ben Sisi as to your grandfather: people say Levi was so holy, that even his donkey refused to eat fodder that hadn't been tithed!"

"Really?" Rachel laughed. "His donkey?" and Rabbi Strabo nodded his head. "So I'd take all this with a grain of salt," he said, his eyes twinkling more than ever.

Chana sighed. "You're a big help," she told her brother, deciding that in the future she would tend to Rachel's education without his assistance.

Fortunately, however, for her pedagogical aspirations, Chana found a more willing collaborator in Tavi, who also felt that it was her duty to instruct the young heathenness and help her mend her pagan ways. This she did in various ways, some more edifying than others. Once, for example, Tavi knocked on the door of Rachel's room and when the girl called out "Who is it?" she came in, bustling with righteous indignation.

"When someone calls at the door," she scolded, "do not say, 'Who is *he* who wishes to enter?' but, 'Who is *she* who wishes to enter?'" and emphasized the feminine pronoun.

And on another occasion Tavi came in clenching a sparkling jewel in one hand, and a ripe blackberry in the other. She opened one hand and showed Rachel the jewel.

"Oh!" said the girl, suitably impressed. But Tavi did not immediately open the other hand, and instead waited till Rachel finished coaxing her in every way she could think of. Then Tavi opened her hand and showed her the crushed berry.

"That'll teach you to be curious!" Tavi said majestically, stalking out of the room and leaving Rachel more puzzled than repentant and not terribly sure just what she had been meant to learn from this little encounter.

Thus, there was much for Rachel to learn during these first few weeks, and not a little that was puzzling and strange to her. But there were other things that she found very much to her liking. The first Sabbath was a revelation. One morning she was roused unusually early and hustled into the kitchen, where a fire was burning brightly in the hearth and a copper tub full of hot water was awaiting her pleasure.

Tavi scrubbed the girl's body till it shone, and then massaged her scalp with fine oils and salves that smelled of flowers and green fields. Chana looked on critically, and smiled her approval as the girl emerged from her bath, her skin glowing pink and clean. Then she was dressed in new garments, and taken to Rabbi Yochanan, the sandler, to be fitted for new shoes. Until now she had gone around in sandals of woven palm fronds, as did most of Nehardea during the work week, but now she was fitted with sandals of fine leather. Rabbi Yochanan measured her foot with deft precision and carefully wrapped the thongs of soft, supple leather around her ankle. When she came back to the house, she peeked into the kitchen and saw Tavi directing the servant girls with unusual briskness - chopping vegetables, braiding loaves of bread, preparing stuffing for the roast meat. But it wasn't till just after sunset, when Chana lit the Sabbath candles, that Rachel realized what was happening that day. She watched, first curious, and then with a feeling she did not know how to define as Chana covered her eyes with her hands, and murmured words that sounded familiar to her. With a shock, she realized that Chana was repeating the same gestures, the same words, that she and Shirin had repeated so many times in the forests back home. *Barukh ata adonai eloheinu melekh haolam. . .* Only now it was no game, and Rachel watched with a feeling akin to awe as the densely-branched trees of the forest vanished before her, and saw how the Sabbath entered the great room and filled it with its presence.

And when the holiday of Purim came around, as it did just a few weeks after her return to Nehardea, the girls clustered together in the high-columned courtyard before the synagogue, as they often did after prayers, and unanimously chose Rachel to be their Purim queen. They crowded around her, explaining Purim and the role of Queen Esther. Esther had saved the Jews! Rachel glowed with happiness at having been chosen. Ah, but Esther was sallow and greenish! Rachel's face fell. "Then why," she asked, "why did the king choose her out of all the other maidens?" Well, *that*, the girls explained, was part of the miracle. "That's not true!" one of the other girls interrupted, on a reproving note, seeing the expression on Rachel's face and hastening to set the record straight. "Esther is likened to a myrtle, or a *hadas*, in the Scroll, not because her skin was greenish, for Heaven's sake, but because, like a myrtle, she had a thread of grace drawn around her, and she was neither too short nor too tall." Rachel relaxed, preferring this version of the Purim miracle, and the girls plied her with further details. Rachel was not quite able to catch everything they said over the babble of voices, but she found herself looking forward happily to Purim, fleetingly recalling the frequent festivities back in Parthia and all the times that she had found herself alone on the sidelines, watching while others rejoiced, solitary amidst the crowds. "I was right," she told herself passionately, "I was right all along. Everything really is going to be different here. This is where I was meant to be."

She related the events of the morning to Chana when she returned home that afternoon, flushed with pride and anticipation. She found her aunt in the kitchen, covered from head to toe in a big apron, rolling out dough in a mist of sunbeams and flour; and Rabbi Strabo, with a rather bemused look on his face, seated comfortably at the kitchen table across from

Pazi, the wife of Rabbi Menachem, who had come in to chat. Chana saw how happy Rachel looked and her heart filled with delight. "Come," she said smiling, handing her niece an apron, "put this on and give me a hand with the baking while you tell me everything." So Rachel wrapped the apron around her while Chana showed her how to cut the dough into triangles and place a dollop of some sweet paste in the center ("poppy-seed," Chana informed her as she experimentally tasted a bit from the tip of her finger), how to fold the corners into little crescents and then to arrange them on the tray alongside the others - "there," Chana said, nodding her chin in the direction of the window sill. Then she did a double take: the tray was empty.

"Why, what happened to the ones I already rolled out?" she asked in amazement. She went closer, as though to make sure the tray really was empty and that the cookies weren't perhaps hiding somewhere, and then putting one hand on the window sill she peered over to see if they could possibly have fallen out. Something wet and warm licked her hand. "Why, it's the neighbor's goat!" she gasped, and then broke into a laugh. The goat licked her hand again and gazed at her with expectant eyes, looking very pleased with itself, and very, very satisfied.

"I was wondering when you'd notice," Rabbi Strabo said mildly.

"Lucky for that goat that Tavi isn't here," Chana remarked, shooing it away with her apron. "You might have said something, Eliezer," and then, without waiting for him to answer, sighed, "Well, we'll just have to start all over again," and sent Rachel off to the miller with a small sack of grain to be ground into flour.

"Make sure he dampens it first," she called out as Rachel went down the street, jingling the coins for the miller in her hand.

Rachel went off in high spirits; she had liked that incident with the goat; it reminded her a bit of home! After all, she had grown up amongst the flocks and the herds; in Parthia she had milked cows almost every day of her life, and at springtime tended countless flocks of goats and sheep in fields alive with bleatings and baas. Of course, goat weren't cows; their eyes weren't so wide and soft, but still, a goat was something, too!

She had to wait a bit at the miller's, for the shop was busy; the whole town, it seemed, was baking for Purim. But she soon fell into conversation with some of the other girls there, one of whom she recognized from synagogue that morning; a pleasant girl with lovely hazel eyes and a long, light-brown braid whose name, she remembered, was Doneg. Doneg introduced the other girl to her as Miriam, adding that the latter had just come back from a visit to Ctesiphon across the river. Miriam was a dark-headed girl, beautifully dressed is a silken *chiton* caught at the shoulder with a jeweled clasp that flashed in the afternoon light. She nodded at Rachel and held out her hand, but there was something in her look that made Rachel sense coming hostilities. She soon discovered that she was right.

"I hear that you were chosen to be Queen Esther this year," Miriam remarked in a non-committal voice. And then, turning to Doneg, "It was my turn, of course, to be Esther, but I don't mind in the least. After all, she's certainly the most Persian of us all."

Rachel did not quite know what she meant, but that Miriam's intent was hostile was clear enough by the way Doneg quickly hushed her up. Doneg then turned to Rachel and began talking about the festivities surrounding Purim: the foods that were baked and the gifts that were exchanged, the reading in synagogue from the Scroll of Esther, and the tremendous racket that the children made whenever the wicked Haman was mentioned. Rachel nodded mechanically at each new item of information but her thoughts were elsewhere, and some of her happiness fled.

She was still churning Miriam's words over in her mind as she walked home; or rather, not her words, so much as the hostility behind them. She hardly saw the houses or the people as she made her way through the narrow alleys. In her mind she was back in the wide, grassy valleys of Parthia, wincing over the remarks of such as Rodoba or Sorhab or any of the other girls who tossed out choice comments from time to time. It was such a little thing, that meeting at the miller's, and yet it filled her with foreboding and a kind of curious dread. Weren't things going to be different here? Was it all going to be the same, after all? She entered the house deep in thought and set the bag of flour down on the table, together with a few silver *zuzim* in change. Everything was just as she left it; the kitchen was warm and inviting, the afternoon sun poured through the windows, but the Rachel who returned was not the Rachel who left, and Chana noticed the difference at once. She broke off a lively conversation with Pazi.

"Did you find the miller's alright?" she asked, cautiously.

Rachel nodded.

"Any trouble finding your way back? I imagine these alleys can be confusing at first."

Rachel shook her head - and then burst into tears. Chana hastily whispered something to Pazi, who rose to her feet and left the house, inwardly regretting that she had to leave that interesting scene behind her. Chana drew Rachel to the table where Rabbi Strabo was sitting aghast, sat her down without speaking, and waited for the storm to pass.

"Rachel," she said, once the tears had finally slowed and she judged it safe to talk, "what happened at the miller's? Did you meet anyone there?"

Rachel hesitated and then nodded. "Yes, two girls, one of whom I'd met before, Doneg, and another girl named Miriam."

At this Chana stiffened and Rabbi Strabo said, "Oho!" and looked very wise and knowing. Rachel went on,

"And she seemed . . . oh, I don't know . . . so hostile to me, so . . ." and her voice trailed off.

"That Doneg!" Chana said angrily, to her brother, sitting bolt upright in her chair. "She *would* think that just because her father –" but Rachel interrupted her aunt here, in order to set the matter straight.

"Not Doneg," she said, shaking her head. "It was Miriam."

"Miriam?" Chana and Rabbi Strabo echoed in unison, both obviously surprised.

Rachel nodded. "Yes, Miriam. Doneg is actually very nice to me whenever we meet." She looked from her aunt to her uncle and then back again. "Why did you think it was Doneg?" she asked curiously.

Chana waved her hand in a vague kind of way. "Oh, it's a long story . . not very important just now," she said, and appeared to lose interest in the whole matter. "If it was just Miriam, I wouldn't worry too much about it, my dear," she said briskly, and then, seeing that Rachel remained downcast, continued in a gentler voice, "It's a shame that there should be such ill-natured people around, but so it is, and there's no getting away from them. *Samuel's daughter*," she added, in a teasing kind of way that was not without firmness, "needn't give it another thought!" At which she got up, and, wrapping the apron back round Rachel's waist, set the girl to rolling out dough and cutting out cookies. She spoke about the coming Purim festivities in the liveliest way, asking questions about Rachel's own role with flattering interest and reminiscing over past celebrations, and as the kitchen filled with the delicious aroma of baking, Rachel felt some of her happiness return.

* * *

More than once, Rabbi Strabo came to take her on various excursions outside Nehardea. The gateways to the city were in disrepair, half-buried in the ground and somewhat hard to push open and making a scraping, protesting sound when they did. But just beyond, the land stretched green and fragrant with orchards, vineyards, and groves of date-palms as far as the eye could see. Shepherds grazed their flocks on the nearby hills, and the dark waters of the Euphrates flowed lazily past the embankments. Rabbi Strabo guided Rachel through the city gates or over them in some places, and pointed out various sights of interest.

"See these palms?" he would ask Rachel, thumping them as proudly as though he had planted them himself. "They've been here since the time of Adam. And those ruins over there on that hill - yes, those over there - why, that was the very castle where the wicked King Nimrod - may his name be blotted out - threw Abraham into the fiery furnace." And Rachel would nod dutifully and look on with proper interest. Despite Chana's best efforts to instruct her, she could not always recall exactly who Adam or Abraham was, or what they were doing in Babylonia in the first place. But by now she knew enough not to ask "Abraham who?" or to expect an Adam or a Moses to be some neighbor or relation.

Rabbi Strabo had conceived the idea of writing a monumental history of Hyrcania, one that would improve - Heaven forgive him - on the descriptions of the great Strabo himself. After all, had Providence not supplied him with a living source? So sometimes, on Sabbath mornings after synagogue, Rabbi Strabo would sit with Rachel in the garden under the shade of the date-palms and listen as the girl obediently answered his questions and told him everything she could possibly remember about her life back in the Gurgan Valley.

"Not," as he earnestly told Rachel, "that I want to be like that historian who spent a whole volume describing the King of King's breeches, or his horse's bit. And also, none of that panegyrical stuff for me. No, indeed! I'll call a fig a fig, and a trough a trough. Don't you think that's the best way?"

"Absolutely," Rachel agreed, nibbling from a huge cluster of grapes. Tavi, muttering about heathenish places and heathenish ways, bustled around them, serving delicious little cakes and slices of sweet melon. Rachel enjoyed sitting there in the little garden behind her aunt's house, surrounded by flowering bushes of pink oleander and shady date-palms with their sprawling leaves. She was accustomed by now to her surroundings, comfortable with her aunt and her new home, but oleanders and palm trees were things she had never seen before coming to Nehardea, and the Gurgan Valley seemed far away as she talked with her uncle, and in a way almost unreal.

One Sabbath morning Chana came home from synagogue somewhat later than usual and found Rachel and Rabbi Strabo busily engaged in his scholarly tasks. Her brother had spread a long scroll across the table and was reading from it to Rachel.

"Pliny says here, no . . . here, that the bratum tree resembles a spreading cypress, that is has very white branches, and that it gives an agreeable scent when burnt."

"Oh yes," Rachel agreed. "It's very pleasant indeed. We sprinkle its leaves into our drinks sometimes, especially on festival days. But I wouldn't say that its branches are white. No, rather a light grey, I should think, or perhaps a kind of pale . . ."

"Oh!" Chana interrupted, startled by the scene before her, and startling Rachel and Rabbi Strabo in turn for neither of them had seen her come in. "Why, Eliezer, what are you doing here still? I heard that the Exilarch came to visit, and that all the men went to Rabbi Nathan's house to hear him speak. Why didn't you go?"

Rabbi Strabo looked guilty. "My foot hurt me," he said.

"You could have put on your good shoes," Chana answered severely.

"It was in the back of the foot."

"You should have put on a sandal."

"There was a puddle in the way."

"You could have crossed it wearing the sandal."

"On the Sabbath?!" he replied, trying to sound indignant. "Don't you agree with what Rabbi Ashi says about wearing sandals on the Sabbath?" Rachel laughed out loud, but Chana continued to look aggrieved.

"Brother," she said to him reprovingly, "you really should have gone. You know that we can't afford to cross the Exilarch now, or to show him any disrespect. The case about Ra-" She broke off suddenly, and looked at her niece with a worried expression. There was a long silence.

"The case about Rachel," the girl said evenly, finishing Chana's sentence for her, and looking exceedingly puzzled. "What about me?"

Chana sighed. She hadn't meant to broach the subject until everything was settled, but perhaps it was time to tell Rachel about the plans being made for her future. She sat down at the table, and patted the seat next to her. "Come sit down next to me," she said kindly.

Rachel moved over and sat beside her aunt. There was a long silence

"Our blessed sages," Chana finally began, "tell us that matches are made in Heaven. And forty days before a child is conceived, a heavenly voice calls out saying 'so-and-so's daughter shall go to so-and-so's son' – or vice versa - so that everyone marries the person to whom he or she is destined."

Rachel listened, greatly interested. She liked the idea very much indeed. Though naturally it had nothing to do with her. Local customs and all that, as Rabbi Strabo always said when she told him about Parthia.

Chana went on. "Your father, may he rest in peace, was a careful father and so before you were born, he betrothed you to the son of the great Rabbi Huna, the Chief Judge of Sura. And his son has grown up to be a fine young man, well-deserving of Samuel's daughter, and so it is my hope that before the end of the year, sometimes towards early autumn, you and Rami will be married."

"Married!" Rachel exclaimed, completely taken aback. This was the last thing she expected.

"Married!" Rabbi Strabo echoed, trying to help. "But we've just begun working on this history, and -"

"Quiet!" Chana commanded him. Your foot hurts." He closed his mouth and Chana went on.

"There are still a few details to work out. For one thing, after you disappeared during the days following the attack of Odenathus, may his name be blotted out -"

"May his name be blotted out," Rachel and Rabbi Strabo repeated mechanically.

"– after you disappeared, as I was saying, Rabbi Huna went and betrothed his son to the daughter of Rabbi Nachman and Yalta. And unfortunately, Yalta is the Exilarch's daughter. But the case will soon be brought to court, and I have no doubt that they will decide in favor of Samuel's daughter - Exilarch or no Exilarch!"

Rachel remained silent. She was thinking of Doneg, Nachman and Yalta's daughter, and things that had rather mystified her suddenly seemed clear. She thought of comments she had heard from other girls, and of the way Doneg had of looking at her, not with anger or hate, but rather in a sad kind of way that had made Rachel wonder more than once. Doneg was a lively, vivacious girl but she had always been kind to her, and she never displayed any of the condescension that Rachel sensed from some of the other girls in town. Indeed, in some ways Doneg reminded her of Shirin, her lively sister back home, and Rachel was inclined to like her.

"But, aunt," Rachel spoke up, rather firmly for her, "I think that Doneg loves that young man, and anyway -"

"Loves him!" Chana exclaimed, rather startled. "What does that have to do with anything? He is your betro-"

"And anyway," Rachel continued, with unusual heat, "I don't want to marry him, or anyone else in fact; and anyway, I'm engaged to Issur back home. It's what my father always wanted."

"Your father!" Chana broke in. "You mean your captor. Samuel's daughter can't go marrying some wild tribesman of Parthia."

"He's not a wild tribesman," Rachel said in a rush of loyalty that would have made Issur's heart pound, if only he knew. "He's a great warrior, and strong and handsome, and he's coming to get me, if I don't go back home first!"

"Yes, those Parthians are good warriors," Rabbi Strabo agreed. "Strabo - or was it Apollodorus? - says that they are fierce looking, with goat-like eyes, handsome beards and long hair, and eyebrows arched in a -"

Chana gave him a pained look and he stopped talking mid-sentence. "Rachel," she said with impressive gravity, "this is your home now, and you must forget those years in Parthia. You are now back where you belong. You must marry, and you must marry one of your own kind. And if I have my way about it, you will marry the son of Rabbi Huna. You are Samuel's daughter!"

Chapter Eight

When Chana told Rachel that little story about matches being made in Heaven, she was speaking the perfect truth. Heavenly voices did determine matches forty days before conception - at least they did in Nehardea. The rabbis all said so. Nevertheless, Chana was a realistic, down-to-earth woman, learned both in books and in the vicissitudes of life, and she well knew that heavenly voices or not, no man could betroth his daughter while she was still a minor and before she gave her agreement; nor his son either, for that matter, before the lad himself could say: 'I wish it.'" The law was very clear on both points. Nevertheless, Chana's hopes were running high: surely Rachel would marry the man chosen for her by her father and assume her rightful place in Nehardea? If Rachel had returned from captivity it could only be through the will of Heaven, and Heaven, having done that much, could scarcely wish her to sink into a position unworthy of Samuel's daughter - there was no sense in that! Nevertheless, Chana was well aware that Nehardea had changed greatly since the days of Samuel and that there were new forces abroad in the land. And so she planned her way carefully.

Rabbi Huna was also in a considerable quandary, and indeed had been ever since the day he first heard that Samuel's daughter had been found somewhere in the wilds of Parthia and brought back to Nehardea. He had rubbed his hands in anxiety upon hearing the news; here was a crisis indeed.

His thoughts flew back to that day - oh so long ago now - when he and Samuel, may he rest in peace, had been sitting together on the banks of the Royal Canal, sipping wine under the willows and enjoying the breeze from the river. The great Rav of Sura had just died, and he, Rabbi Huna, was generally considered to be Rav's spiritual heir and the man most likely to take over the orphaned Academy in Sura.

It was a fine day, and Samuel, for his part, had also started thinking. Did he grieve the death of Rav? It was hard to say. Certainly Rav had been a great scholar, and when Samuel first heard of his death, people said he tore thirteen suits of clothing as a sign of mourning. But there was no denying that while Rav was alive, Samuel had torn an even greater numbers of garments in sheer frustration with that worthy sage. If he, Samuel, ruled one way, Rav was sure to rule just the other. If he decided that a certain type of oil was kosher, Rav decided that it was not; if he included certain words in a prayer, Rav discarded them, and so on and so forth. Despite all the tension, however, the two sages also felt a genuine respect for each other and tried hard - perhaps too hard - to show it. Samuel still winced when he recalled the time that he and Rav had practically come to blows at the entrance of the synagogue - each of them attempting to give precedence to the other - and how they had both ended up wedged in the door. But Rav was dead now, and the days of rivalry were over and done with.

It was a fine sunny day there on the banks of the Royal Canal, and Samuel was feeling at peace with the world. So he turned to Rabbi Huna and said, "You know, my wife is about to have another child. If it is a girl, let her be betrothed to your son Rami. Let bygones be bygones. What could be better than joining the Academy of Nehardea with that of Sura?"

"Alas," said Rabbi Huna, "I am as vinegar to wine compared to Rav - may he rest in peace -"

"May he rest in peace," Samuel echoed.

"- but your suggestion does me honor, and who am I to reject such a noble alliance?" So the two men betrothed Samuel's as yet unborn daughter to the not yet three-year-old Rami. And pleased with their day's work, the two men then rose and went their separate ways.

Truly it is said that what man proposes, God disposes. Samuel's wife indeed gave birth to a daughter, Rachel, but Samuel himself died only a few months before the child was born. And then, when the little girl was only four years old she disappeared during the invasion of Odenathus - may his name be blotted out - and was given up for dead. So when Rabbi Nachman approached Rabbi Huna in the years following these terrible events, there seemed to be no reason why he should not betroth his Rami to Nachman's daughter, Doneg. Indeed, the idea had pleased Rabbi Huna not a little. After all, Rabbi Nachman was the son-in-law of the Exilarch, and though Rabbi Huna had of course esteemed Samuel greatly, what greater honor could befall his family?

It was, therefore, with no little dismay that Rabbi Huna received the news that Samuel's daughter had returned to Nehardea. Word of the event struck Huna like lightning while he was out taking his usual walk just before nightfall, making the rounds of his fields and vineyards. Huna enjoyed these evening strolls though the fragrant fields, watching as his tenants pruned the vineyards and talking things over with the farmers who cultivated his land.

Huna had come far in life. Though he could claim a noble descent - his own great-great-grandfather having been the Exilarch himself back in the days of Judah the Prince - he had grown up in poverty, and the years of want could never seem distant enough for his peace of mind. Take that incident just last week, for example. There he was, celebrating the wedding of his son, Rabbah, greeting his guests at the door and collecting the silken cloaks of his daughters and daughters-in-law as they entered the house. Soon the heaps of silk all but hid him from view, so that Chova, his wife, had looked for him in vain. Of course, this was because Huna was such a short man, and everyone in the room laughed at the incident. But Huna could not help recalling that day so many years ago in Sura when he, an impoverished young newly-wed, had stood before the Head of the Academy on the eve of the Sabbath, explaining in embarrassment why he was girded in rope for the holy day.

"But where is your fine sash?" Rav asked. "The silk one you usually wear?"

"Well," Huna replied, as matter-of-fact as he could, "I had to sell it in order to buy wine for the Sabbath blessing."

Rav looked silently at his beloved pupil for a few moments and then said gently, and with only a hint of a smile, "If so, may you one day be covered in silk from head to toe."

Well - Rav's words have come true, Huna thought wryly that night as his wife, laughing, had come to his rescue. He was covered in silk, indeed, and as wealthy as he could ever have dreamed. But the years of plenty had not been able to erase the years of dearth. He remembered the times when people had had to come out to the fields where he was grazing his cattle, and pay him for time lost in order to persuade him to settle their cases. Or when, up in the date-palm gathering the fruit, he would agree to adjudicate only if someone else would come up to take his place. Of course, people had always been willing to do so, so much did they value his knowledge of the law and the wisdom of his judgment.

Just where his great wealth came from nobody knew: some people attributed it to his great wisdom and knowledge; others averred that he had found buried treasure, but whatever the source one thing was certain, and that was that Huna's wealth greatly increased over the years, along with his reputation for scholarship. In addition to the court over which he presided all year long at Sura, he held special lessons twice a year, in early spring and autumn, when there was little to be done out in the fields, and Jews thirsty for knowledge had time to travel to Sura and sit at his feet. So popular were these lessons that during these two months no less than eight hundred students ever sat down at his table to eat. And - people joked - when they rose from their meals, they raised such a dust that the sun was nearly blotted out, and over in the Land of Israel people were said to remark: "Ah! it's only Rabbi Huna's students getting up from the table."

Despite all his wealth and renown, or perhaps even because of it, Huna never lost the feeling that his good fortune in life was only a lucky accident and that it behooved him, therefore, to act with great piety and to multiply good deeds. Thus when it turned out one year that the vintage produced four hundred barrels of sour wine, he immediately declared a personal fast and doubled his kindnesses to his tenants. It was also said that he personally financed the reconstruction of many a tumbled-down wall throughout the vicinity of Sura, and that whenever he had a meal, he flung his doors open wide for one and all to enter.

But for all his humility, Huna was too honest not to realize that he had been flattered when Rabbi Nachman suggested an alliance between their families through the marriage of Rami and Doneg. Who could have known that Rachel would come back after so many years? Such a thing had never happened before. And in truth, Huna admitted to himself, he preferred to let the alliance with the Exilarch's family go through. The years of want, of that aching desire for dignity and honors, could not be forgotten so easily as to renounce this alliance with the Exilarch's family. Huna wanted to do the right thing, and yet his path was not clear before him.

Chana, for her part, knew all of Huna's apprehensions and fears; knew them as surely as if he had told them to her himself. She knew that despite his great wealth he was haunted by memories of poverty, and also that he truly desired to do what was right. But she also knew Rabbi Nachman, and she realized, therefore, that it would be necessary to help Huna along the right path. It was for this reason that she started procedures for looking into Rachel's inheritance and finding out what remained to the girl after all these long years. This would not be easy: Rabbi Nachman was not only interested in the affair; he was also the Chief Judge of Nehardea and it was in his court that Rachel's rights would have to be fought.

* * *

It was somewhere about this time that Rachel came home one day to find Chana and several of the neighbors seated around the kitchen table that gave onto the courtyard, listening attentively to Rabbi Strabo who was standing and reading out loud from something that looked like a letter. Even Tavi, busy with her pots and pans and flushed from the heat of the oven, seemed to be listening. She was greeted by a buzz of excited voices.

"Here's Rachel!" Pazi cried out, spying the girl as soon as she walked in the room.

"Oh, Rachel," Chana said, smiling, "here's a letter from your sisters!" Rachel flushed with pleasure. These were the sisters of whom she had heard so much since her return to Nehardea. The two sisters who had seen their mother killed and gone into captivity crying their sister's name, and then been taken by pirates to the Land of Israel. There, in the great town of Sepphoris on the shores of the Sea of Galilee, they had acted with great presence of mind, leaving their captors to loiter outside the synagogue while they went in and claimed to be undefiled captives. In all this they showed such unerring dexterity, such knowledge of the fine points of Jewish law, that the scholars there instantly realized that these must be the daughters of a rabbi. And upon learning that the two girls were none other than the daughters of Samuel, may he rest in peace, the renowned sage from far-off Babylonia, they quickly paid the pirates their ransom and then - lest the girls again fall into evil hands - married them off to two of the young scholars there.

Rachel could not really remember her two sisters; even their names sounded strangely in her ears, and yet she was somehow sure that these were the women whose presence had flashed through her memory the night of that fateful meeting with the two foreign merchants. She had longed to hear from them ever since returning to Nehardea, for they were the missing link with her childhood; the sisters who could testify to what she had been before that terrible day of destruction. So she turned eagerly now towards her uncle and sat down at the table, her heart pounding with anticipation.

Chana saw her eagerness and gave her an affectionate smile. "Eliezer," she said, turning to her brother, "start over again so Rachel can hear," and so Rabbi Strabo, clearing his throat, obediently went back to the beginning. Rachel sat at the table, chin in hand, oblivious to everything except her uncle's voice:

> *To our darling sister Rachel, who has returned from captivity: Peace, peace and all the blessings of Heaven upon thee. May the Lord's blessings fall upon thy head like the gentle rain, and be like the fishes in the sea or the stars in the sky for number. How long have we, thy loving sisters in the land of milk and honey, mourned for thee: lifting our eyes in the hope of hearing of you, crying for you as a woman cries in the travails of birth, longing for you as the earth longs for rain. Whenever we remembered thee our hearts sank, our knees trembled; yea, our very souls shriveled with grief. And now the joyful tidings are heard upon the hills: "Rachel, the daughter of Samuel, hath returned from captivity!" Praised be He who brings back the dead.*

"Back from the dead?" Rachel interrupted, somewhat taken aback. But Chana quickly hushed her up and Rabbi Strabo read on:

O for the wings of the dove, that we might fly to thee in Nehardea, and see our beloved sister and there be joined to her again! But alas, our feet are chained –

"'Chained'? Why 'chained'?" Rachel echoed, amazed, but her uncle's voice rolled on:

- and we fear we cannot visit thee. Our heart flies to thee on eagles' wings, and our husbands and children - may the Lord bless them forever - and especially my little Rachel, join us in sending our love to the sister who is forever enshrined in our heart. May you soon forget all thy sorrows and grief. And may the Lord send thee a choice youth of Israel to lead you under the wedding canopy, that thou mayest be as a fruitful bough in the garden of the Lord. Amen amen. From thy loving sisters Sarah and Deborah, here in the Holy Land of Israel.

"Now that's what I call a nice letter," said Pazi, in a satisfied voice, while Chana and the other neighbors nodded in agreement and Tavi surreptitiously wiped her eyes with her apron. Rabbi Strabo folded the letter into a triangle and placed it on the table, beaming at Rachel all the while.

"I didn't understand a word of it," Rachel declared, rather mutinously. "Except that they seem to have decided I was dead." She picked up the letter from the table, turning it this way and that in her hands, as though in doing so she might shake out its real meaning. Surely her uncle had left something out? Memories of her childhood, of their parents, of their home? But turn it around as she would, the elegant missive refused to yield its secrets. She put the letter back down in despair.

"But isn't it somewhat . . . somewhat . . ." she asked, groping for the right word. Six pairs of eyes looked reproachfully at her.

"It's a very nice letter," Chana said reprovingly, "and written in the very best style. I'm sure they paid a lot of money for it!"

"Paid?" Rachel asked, surprised. "They paid someone to write it for them?"

"Why, of course," Chana replied. "That's what letter-writers are for. Haven't you ever seen Rabbi Hamnuna in the market-place? He's the one who sits under that big palm tree just past the weavers' shops - surely you've noticed him?"

Indeed, Rachel *had* noticed Rabbi Hamnuna, and also the crowd of women who usually huddled around him, following with their eyes every word that he wrote. But only now did she fully understand what he did there.

"Oh," she said, thoughtfully, digesting the information.

"But you needn't go to him if you want to answer your sisters," her uncle assured her. "I'll write the letter for you." And seeing the look of chagrin on her face gallantly added, "And nary a word about Strabo!" but Rachel just shook her head. That wouldn't do at all. What she wanted to ask her sisters, she didn't want her uncle or Chana to hear.

The next day towards sunset, Rachel wrapped a warm woolen shawl around her shoulders and left the house, supposedly on her way to synagogue to hear evening prayers, but in reality bent on the market place in search of Rabbi Hamnuna. If her sisters went to letter-writers, so could she! She threaded her way past the stands of butchers and carpenters, gold-smiths and silver-smiths, basket-makers and weavers in linen, silk and wool, and found Rabbi Hamnuna in his usual place beneath the giant date-palm; an old and very scholarly-looking man in a flowing robe and a white skullcap. He was seated cross-legged on a faded old rug of many colors, head studiously bent as he traced the characters across a sheet of parchment, while a woman looked anxiously on. Rachel noticed that Rabbi Hamnuna had effectively turned the great palm into his office, or rather into his office, table, and chair all in one. He used the rough ledges of the trunk as shelves to hold his skins and parchment; he hung the various tools of his trade from the spiky points of the bast, as though they were nails; and he had even wrapped some cushions around the prickly trunk of the tree with a piece of rope, to make it comfortable for his back. The sight of such professionalism rather intimidated Rachel, and she waited her turn in silence. Eventually Rabbi Hamnuna finished the letter, and looking back up he handed it to the woman and graciously accepted a few coins from her hand. The woman left in a flurry of blessings and thank-yous, leaving Rachel quite alone with the scribe. But Rabbi Hamnuna seemed in no hurry to notice her. He sharpened his quill with a knife and stirred his ink, added a few drops of what looked like olive oil to the opaque black mixture, and only then condescended to ask Rachel her business.

Assuming a look of self-confidence that she hoped belied her thumping heart, Rachel asked, "Will you write a letter for me?" and nervously jingled the coins in her hand. At this the man looked up alertly and gazed at her hand, apparently calculating the number of coins behind those closed fingers.

He picked up a pen. "Three *zuzim*. Hebrew or Aramaic?" he asked.

"I was thinking of Persian," Rachel said, rather taken aback. The letter-writer did not seem to approve of this answer, but he dipped his pen into the ink nevertheless, and smoothed a fresh sheet of parchment across his tablet.

"Yes?" he inquired in a business-like manner, his pen poised in the air.

"To my dear sisters in the Land of Israel," Rachel began, flustered a bit by that look of disapproval. "I was so happy to receive your letter yesterday, and hope that this letter in reply finds you and your families in very good health." She paused for breath, and the scribe read back:

> *To my dear sisters, the light of mine eyes, who dwell in the holy Land of Israel, greetings from one who prays to the Lord for thy well-being, and who received thy epistle flowing in words as sweet as honey.*

The man paused and scratched out the last word, muttering to himself, " 'nectar;' perhaps 'nectar' is better." He made the correction and then looking back up he waited, pen in hand, for Rachel to continue. Rachel, a bit startled, did so:

"I was so sorry to hear that you have been grieving for me all these years! Especially since I wasn't dead at all, or even in captivity. You see, I was adopted by a very nice family, who cared for me as a daughter and brought me up in the mountain valleys of Parthia. I also learned how to ride a horse, and to shoot arrows, and to milk a cow - none of which the girls here seem to do." Rachel stopped, and gave the letter-writer a quizzical look. He obediently read back:

Thy grief is my grief, and truly, I learned heathen ways amongst the idolaters. Blessed be the Lord who brings back the dead.

"But that's not at all what I said!" Rachel protested, amazed.

"Of course not," the man said placidly, looking over the letter in a pleased way. "That's why you're paying me to write this letter - you *are* paying me, aren't you?" he asked anxiously.

"Yes, of course I'm paying you," Rachel said impatiently, "but please write exactly what I say." The scribe looked decidedly hurt but he gave a reluctant nod, so Rachel collected her thoughts and went on:

"My dear sisters, what I wish to ask you is this: is it not true that as a little girl I was very mischievous, and that I made friends with everyone who came to the house, even the children of the servants? And that I climbed trees and got scratched by rose-bushes? You see, when I was in Parthia I was rather . . ."

The man scribbled on, dipping his pen in the ink from time to time, and then read back the words almost exactly as Rachel had said them, though it clearly pained him to do so.

Rachel listened, nodding her head at the end of each sentence, and adding a few more lines which the scribe again read back to her word for word. There was a brief spat over a sentence beginning "O for the wings of an eagle . . ." - "I can't say that!" Rachel objected, "that's what they said to me!" - but after a bit of grumbling he scraped it away and read the rest of the letter to Rachel's satisfaction.

"Now sign it 'from your loving sister Rachel, here in the holy community of Nehardea,' " she instructed him.

"Wouldn't you like to ask them about the Ten Lost Tribes?" the scribe inquired, looking up. "It's only one *zuz* extra, and it's all the rage nowadays." But Rachel just firmly shook her head "no". Sighing, the scribe ended the letter as bidden and put it into the girl's hand. Rachel handed him the three coins, thanked him for the letter and turned to leave, but the man stopped the girl in her tracks. "Now look here!" he said, angrily, "You owe me two more *zuzim*!"

"But you said it was three *zuzim* - not five!" Rachel protested.

"Three for the base price - but there were lots of extras; the Persian, you know, and then all that polishing up at the beginning. Two *zuzim* please!"

"You said *three*!" Rachel repeated, getting angry. "Three altogether! And I didn't *want* my letter polished up!"

"No?" said the scribe, and snatched the paper out of her hand. "If you don't appreciate good writing," he said huffily, "you don't have to take it. Don't think you're the only returned captive around! There's p-l-e-n-t-y of others for whom it'll do just fine - I'll just scrape away these last lines...", and flinging the coins back at her, suited action to words. And as Rachel flounced away he called out spitefully, "It was a silly letter anyway!"

A silly letter! The words floated past Rachel as she turned on her heel and left the market place, hardly noticing the noisy clamor of craftsmen and shopkeepers as they hurriedly closed up for the night, intent upon reaching synagogue in time for evening prayer. A silly letter! When she had waited so long to ask those questions, and when the answers meant so much to her! But as she walked slowly home in the early winter darkness, lifting her face to a sky alive with stars and feeling the cool breeze in her hair, her thoughts gradually calmed down, and her heart ceased beating in that thumping, erratic way. Something of her usual equilibrium returned, and she felt a smile playing around her lips. A silly letter! Well, maybe it had been, after all. What did the past really matter? What mattered now was the future.

Chapter Nine

Despite Rachel's brave words about the past as she walked home that night, the past mattered more than she knew, and the future - her future - had in some ways been shaped by a past of which she had no concept or knowledge.

Some forty years before Rachel's time, before anyone had ever imagined that desert scourge called Odenathus, King of Palmyra, Nehardea had been one of the most thriving centers of trade in the Tigris-Euphrates Valley, and as Shulamit, Rachel's mother, made her way towards the synagogue one winter evening to bring her father the woolen cape he had absently forgotten earlier in the day, she happened to pass a small caravan of camels kneeling under a cluster of date-palms. Perhaps it was not *quite* a caravan; there were only some three or four camels kneeling there in the shadows, but clearly they had just come off the caravan route, for they were covered with dust and their burdens emitted that hot, windy scent of the desert. As the daughter of a merchant she had an eye for these things, and for a moment she wondered whence they had come. But only for a moment; such sights were too common in Nehardea to awaken much interest in Shulamit's seventeen-year-old heart, and she never would have given that caravan more than a passing thought had it not been for a small incident that occurred at that moment. Just as she was going past the camels, one of the bales piled high on their backs slipped out of the ropes securing it in place, and falling to the ground, spilled some of its contents into the street. A bolt of cloth rolled towards her, unfurling a length of satin brocade as it went, and automatically, as though she were playing ball with her younger brothers, she quickened her steps and stopped it with her foot. A man disengaged himself from the shadows and ran over to Shulamit, who had in the meantime picked the runaway cloth up in her arms and was attempting to rewind the material as much as she could, but the bolt was heavy and difficult for her to manage.

"Here, I'll take that," the man said contritely, removing the heavy burden from her arms. "Thank you so much - you stopped it like a pro. I'll bet you have little brothers at home."

"Why, yes, I do," Shulamit replied, still looking down at the battered cloth and attempting to smooth the rumpled folds. It was a beautiful piece of satin, purple or perhaps dark blue in color - it was hard to tell under starlight - and embroidered with flowers; fantastical flowers such as Shulamit knew had never been seen on God's green earth. Delicately, she touched one of the silken petals with the tip of her finger. "It's beautiful," she said, somewhat wistfully, handing the cloth over, and as she did so she looked up into the man's face. Her heart skipped a beat. It was the handsomest face she had ever seen, dark and firmly chiseled, and for a moment she felt as though she could scarcely breathe.

"Yes," the man said, but he wasn't looking at the cloth. There was a moment of silence, and then murmuring something between "thank you" and "you're welcome," or maybe "goodbye," Shulamit fled towards the synagogue and left the man and his camels behind her.

She could have left her father's cloak with the sexton and gone back home, but instead she sat down in a far corner of the benches that lined the synagogue walls and listened to the evening prayer-service. The last thing she wanted was to go past that caravan again; the camels, no doubt, would be there till the moon rose. She did not hear a word of the service nor had she really thought that she would; all she wanted was to sit quietly and regain her composure, for she could feel the hot blood in her face and her heart was thumping erratically. But the only thing she could think of was that bolt of satin brocade unrolling towards her like some gorgeous carpet, and the man's face looking down at her in the darkness.

After prayers, she joined her father on the steps of the synagogue and handed him the cloak, which the evening chill made very welcome. Rabbi Yair thanked his daughter for her thoughtfulness, and resuming the conversation with two of his fellow-worshippers, walked slowly in the direction of home. Shulamit trailed silently behind them.

As they neared the camels, Shulamit edged closer to her father, as closely as she could without drawing his attention to her, but it proved to be a useless precaution. For no sooner did they approach than the stranger darted into the street and grasped her father's hand in a formal gesture of greeting, his hand on his heart in the manner of Syrians. Rabbi Yair, needless to say, did not introduce her to the stranger, nor did the two men talk long, but when they parted Shulamit saw that the man's eyes flickered in her direction for just a moment.

"Well, that was well-met," her father said in a pleased voice, to his friends. "Lajash is one of the merchants of the firm I do business with in Hatra, and that caravan was just late enough in returning to Nehardea to make me think I ought to start worrying."

"Well-met, indeed," replied Levi ben Sisi, a neighbor and friend who had only recently moved to Nehardea from the Land of Israel. "What says the merchant?"

"Oh, he'll give me all the details tomorrow, when he comes to pay his accounts," Yair replied. "But the caravan seems to have been successful enough." And with that the group reached the crossroads and separated, each man turning towards his own home, and Shulamit and her father walked the rest of the way in silence under the starry winter sky.

It was some time after this incident that Chana, Shulamit's sister and the eldest daughter in the family, made a visit to the paternal mansion after having been absent for a few weeks due to the illness of first one and then another of her children. Chana had made a splendid marriage; her husband Phineas was the son of Abba ben Abba, one of the leading Jewish dignitaries in Nehardea, and a man known as much for his great wealth as for his piety and good deeds. Like his father, Phineas dealt in silks, which he imported from China (or from "the Jade-Gate itself," as Phineas liked to put it) and then reexported to the cities along the Syrian coast. He was a kind man and an enterprising merchant, but as a young girl Chana had dreamed of marrying a great scholar, one who would be immersed in Torah and Jewish law. She even dreamed of marrying the head of one of the leading academies of Jewish learning that were scattered throughout Babylonia, and at the height of her daydreams debated in her own heart the respective merits of Sura over Pumbedita, or of Mechoza over Nisibis. But when Abba ben Abba suggested an alliance between the two houses, her father, Yair, was only too happy to agree to a marriage between his daughter, Chana, and the up-and-coming young merchant, Phineas.

Chana and Phineas had been duly married and then blessed with two sons; one daughter, alas, had died in infancy. As a busy merchant, Phineas did not have much time for study, but though pious and observant of the Law he was content to leave the honors of the Torah to Samuel, his older brother and the true scholar in the family. Samuel had already gained a considerable reputation in the field of civil law, and people pointed to him as one destined for greatness. "Alas that he remains unmarried," they unfailingly added, "for surely that is the only obstacle to his career." And so on and so forth, for Nehardea was a small town for all of its big-city ways, and everyone knew everybody else's business, and commented accordingly.

And on this Sabbath day, Chana and her family received a royal welcome in the paternal home, as though it had been months rather than weeks since their last visit there. There were questions to ask and questions to answer; cakes to eat and cakes to refuse; and the saga of her children's illness to be related moment by moment and detail by detail. But in the midst of all the cheerful activity, Chana found herself glancing at Shulamit time and again. She was older than her sister by a number of years, and tended to worry about her with all the solicitude of a mother.

"What's wrong with her?" Chana wondered to herself. "Or rather, what's so right? She looks radiant; almost glowing with happiness." Chana sought enlightenment from her mother. "Has Shulamit been betrothed?" she asked, trying to get to the root of the mystery. But Mother shook her head. Father, she informed Chana, was very busy these days and so they had decided to put off any talk about marriage for Shulamit till the autumn.

"Shulamit is looking very happy," Chana said cautiously, trying another route.

"Why, she's happy to see the children looking so well after their illness!" her mother beamed. Not much enlightenment here, Chana decided, so she changed the subject and talked about other matters, inwardly determining on a chat later on with Shulamit herself. But as it turned out, there was no need for Chana to ask Shulamit anything at all.

Just before dinner a young man appeared at the house, and within two seconds Chana knew everything there was to know. If previously she thought Shulamit glowing, she now saw her positively radiant, and more beautiful than she had ever seen her before. As beautiful as a bride, Chana found herself thinking, and then caught herself up short. Who was this man? Clearly, he was not Jewish. She looked at him sharply; a handsome, dark-skinned man of somewhat more than medium height, probably from Syria, or perhaps the Lebanon, with flashing black eyes and a powerful build. And what was worse, he was clearly in love with her sister. The two barely greeted each other when he came in, for Shulamit looked down at his entrance, obviously flustered and shy, but Chana saw that when they did finally speak for a moment, their eyes gave them away. Chana looked around the room. What was wrong with everybody? Couldn't they see what was happening right under their noses?

Introductions were duly made. "Lajash?" echoed Chana, stumbling over the unfamiliar name.

"Lajash," he confirmed, smiling, and Shulamit added her bit. "It's the name of kings," she said, and then blushed, looking more radiant than ever. "It would be," Chana thought to herself grimly, and followed her mother out to the kitchen at the very first opportunity. Oh, yes, her mother replied, smiling. Lajash had already dined with them on several occasions - such a charming young man, don't you think? Alas, Chana *did* think so, and she became more worried than ever; clearly, Lajash was a welcome guest in that house.

"So how many times has he been here?" she asked. Her mother thought it over, and began reckoning up the different times on her fingers. She had just reached the fourth finger when a question from the cook forced her to turn her attention to issues of a more culinary nature.

"So he's visited the house at least four times," Chana said to herself, auguring the worst. "Four times *at least*, and probably more."

Chana could find no fault with Lajash. Over dinner he listened politely as Phineas waxed eloquent on the subject of Hatra, for upon learning that the stranger came from the famed caravan city, Phineas launched into a detailed description of the city he had once visited, as travelers will. He described the thronging market-place and caravanserai, the great temples to the gods of the Sun and the Moon, rich with gold and ivory, and all with as much enthusiasm as though he, Phineas, were the native of Hatra and Lajash the stranger to its wonders. Lajash listened good-naturedly to this travelogue about the city in which he had been born and raised, and only once ventured a remark.

"And," Phineas continued, describing the rounded walls of the city with an eloquent swish of his fork, "and besides that, it also has one hundred and - Oh, dear, what was that number, Chana, one hundred and twenty? forty? - "

"One hundred and sixty, I believe," supplied Lajash, politely.

"Yes, that's it; one hundred and sixty towers *and* four different exits, each one leading to one of the four different trade-routes." Greatly to his credit, Lajash managed to look impressed by the words of his host's son-in-law, without making him look ridiculous at the same time. No, Chana could find no fault with him. "Come, Phineas," she said, with a meaningful look. "It's time we were going home."

Chana had taken an active role in the conversation at dinner, but in the secret recesses of her mind she was worrying about her sister. What should she do? She couldn't say anything to her parents; that would be to accuse Shulamit. She couldn't say anything to Shulamit; Shulamit was a dreamer, and opposition might only push that particular dream closer to reality. But by the time she and Phineas returned home that night, she had decided on a course of action. And, being Chana, she lost no time in putting the plan into motion.

"Phineas," she said at length, after she had put her two young sons to bed for the night and returned alone to her husband, "Phineas, you'll never guess what Shulamit told me this afternoon."

"Hmmm," he answered absently, tired from the pleasures of the table and more than ready for bed himself. He was in no mood for guessing.

"She told me that she was in love with Samuel."

"With Samuel?" Phineas asked, somewhat more alertly. "With my brother?"

"With your brother Samuel," Chana confirmed, and watched covertly to see his reaction. There wasn't any, and Chana sighed in disappointment. But a few days later, when her hopes in this ruse had all but faded, Phineas came home in a bustle and she learned that her stratagem had succeeded after all.

"Well," he said, with an air of obvious importance, "it's *you* this time who will never guess!"

"Guess about what?" Chana asked, absently.

"Why, guess what Samuel said today."

Chana sat up straight. "I can't guess," she said, not entirely truthfully, for her head was spinning with conjectures. She sat at the table and looked questioningly at her husband, outwardly calm but inwardly anxious; just yesterday she had seen that man, handsomer than ever, enter her parents' house again.

"Well, what did he say?" she queried.

Phineas took a deep breath and looked important. "Remember what you told me the other night about your sister?"

Chana made a show of not remembering, and then, as though after a great effort, she said, "Oh! you mean about Shulamit being in love with your brother?"

"Exactly!" Phineas said, triumphantly. "I told Samuel that Shulamit was in love with him." He paused.

"And he said -?" Chana said, encouragingly.

"And he said, 'You mean Chana's sister, the one with the curly brown hair?'"

"Yes?" Chana breathed. "And then what?"

"Oh, that was all," Phineas replied, and Chana sat back in her chair, considerably deflated. But Phineas was not quite finished. "That is, that's all he said to *me*. But afterwards he went up to Father and said to him, 'Get me this damsel to wife!'"

"He did?" Chana said, truly astonished; first and foremost by Samuel's lover-like impetuosity - who would have thought he had it in him? - and second, by the ease with which her plans had borne fruit. Indeed, she had never thought it would all be so easy, and she was as surprised and happy as if she had not planned the whole thing herself. "Thank God," was all she could think. "Thank God. This will be the saving of Shulamit."

"He did, indeed," Phineas assured her, and mimicking his brother's voice he said again, "'Get me this damsel to wife!'" and laughed a little at the memory. "Just like one of the Patriarchs!"

But in the end, things were not so easy after all, and Chana experienced more than a little anxiety before the day finally came in which she saw Samuel and Shulamit actually standing beneath the wedding canopy. The wedding ceremony of which all Nehardea rejoiced to hear did not, in the end, take place on its first appointed day, for the bride fell mortally ill at the very height of the preparations. Needless to say, Shulamit's sudden illness was the subject of more than a few whispers here and there, for not everyone understood that Samuel's great learning more than made up for whatever shortcomings he might have in his physical appearance. Indeed, there were those who whispered the word "poison," but others, shocked by such talk, quickly opposed the idea. "After all," they pointed out, "no girl can be married against her will - the rabbis themselves say so. Take poison? What nonsense. Why, all she had to do was refuse." But in their hearts they knew better. For who, in fact, had ever heard of a girl refusing the groom chosen for her by her parents? Certainly no one they knew.

Chana saw Lajash one last time, a few weeks after Shulamit's formal betrothal to Samuel. It was in the marketplace, where he was loading packs onto a string of kneeling camels; apparently stocking up for the journey back to Hatra. Chana had to walk past him twice before she could be sure that it really was Lajash, so changed was he from the last time they had met. But it was Lajash, indeed, somber and silent, and she hurried on lest he should look up and see her.

And it was this final glimpse which haunted Chana in the years thereafter. For only a few months after Lajash left, word of Hatra's destruction filtered back to Nehardea: King Shapur and his troops had razed the rebellious city to the ground and put its citizens to the sword. Had Lajash been amongst the victims, Chana wondered? Was Shulamit waiting for him to return? And how much, exactly, had Shulamit heard of Hatra's late tragedy? Chana spent much of her time tending Shulamit in her sick-room, but although her final glimpse of Lajash gnawed at her heart she never broached the subject of Lajash with her sister, and she never regretted what she had done. In her eyes, Shulamit was as a brand rescued from the fire.

In later years, Chana almost managed to convince herself that it was not from a broken heart that Shulamit had almost died that time. After all, she argued with herself, Shulamit had only mentioned Lajash's name once during that entire period - and only during her wildest delirium, at that. And after she married Samuel, moreover, she seemed contented enough with her life; proud of her husband, who indeed became one of the greatest leaders of Babylonian Jewry, and content with her home and her children.

And if she never again saw Shulamit look as radiant as she had that day in her father's home, when she had slowly raised her eyes to Lajash - well, such was the way of the world, and one could only bless God, and go on.

* * *

Chana, then, had loved her sister, and Rachel's return to Nehardea meant a great deal to her; indeed, was little short of a miracle in her eyes. She had been moved to tears when she saw how like her mother Rachel was, and she had wept again that first Sabbath eve when she saw Rachel whispering the blessing over the lights along with her, for she realized that Rachel had remembered the words to the prayer throughout the years of captivity. But, as we have also seen, Chana was nothing if not a practical woman, and even as she wept she was making plans for Rachel's future. She wanted to see Rachel happily settled in life, and for Chana, as for any other matron of her acquaintance, this meant happily married. And more specifically, it meant happily married to the son of Rabbi Huna, just as Samuel had intended himself.

It was not that Chana sought to undo the past by this marriage, or to deny the changes that had overtaken the family in the years since Nehardea's destruction: Chana was neither sentimental enough nor even, perhaps, sufficiently imaginative to think in such terms. The past could not be undone. Samuel was dead, and the luster of his fame had long since dimmed in the eyes of these busy, bustling Nehardeans, absorbed in rebuilding their city and fortunes in the wake of the destruction by Odenathus. Chana herself was quite willing to sink into the role that fate had allotted her and remain in the eyes of her fellow townsmen a widow who had seen better days; a woman who had known wealth and power but whose sun had set. But Rachel! That was something else altogether. Rachel was the daughter of Samuel, the first of all sages and a companion of kings. Rachel's sisters, it is true, had been forced to make do with husbands of lesser merit, for although Samuel's name had been respected in the Land of Israel, it did not carry the same prestige that it did here in Babylonia. The rabbis in Sepphoris had paid lip service to "greatness fallen," and solemnly compared the world to a water-wheel in a garden, now full and now empty, now rising, now falling. But when the time came to marry the girls off, they had thought second-row scholars good enough for Samuel's daughters. But Rachel was here in Babylonia where Samuel had been known and revered, and she deserved to marry into one of the first families of Babylonian Jewry.

In point of fact, Chana thought, what *but* this marriage could counter the influences of those years spent in the wilds of Parthia, or transform the returned captive into a pious Jewish matron? And transform her not only in the eyes of their neighbors, but in those of Rachel herself? For Chana saw that docile as Rachel was, and eager to learn the ways of her family, those years amongst the heathens had taken their toll. She saw how her eyes wistfully followed the horses when the desert Arabs rode into town, and the flocks of sheep and goats when they went out to pasture in the early morning hours. And she saw that Rachel not only fumbled with her prayer-book - that was natural enough considering how short a time she had been here - but she also seemed indifferent when Chana tried to explain to her the intricacies of synagogue rite and prayer, and at times, alas, even bored. And perhaps most important, she saw that Rachel was shy with the girls who should have been her friends by now, somewhat aloof and awkward, and she attributed this - wrongly, as it happened - to a sense of inferiority natural to a girl brought up amongst heathens when suddenly faced with a reflection of what she herself should have been. Not that Chana had anything against the followers of Zoroaster. Indeed, Chana considered herself a tolerant woman. She never heeded Tavi's misanthropic remarks about fire-worshippers, and indeed enjoyed cordial relations with a number of Zoroastrians here in Nehardea. But she was unable to imagine an alternate life for herself; any life which swerved one iota from the Jewish values she knew; and hence she was unable to imagine one for Rachel, either, or to imagine that Rachel might possibly conceive of one for herself. She had been amazed when once, some few weeks after Rachel's arrival in Nehardea, her neighbor Pazi asked Rachel if she had wanted to come back to Nehardea?

"What kind of fool's question is that?" Chana had said to herself, indignantly, and indeed nearly said so out loud. *Of course* Rachel had wanted to come back; how could she not? How could Samuel's daughter not have languished amongst the wilds of Parthia or yearned, day after day, for a rich Jewish life amongst her own people? In some hazy corner of her subconscious, Chana always envisioned Rachel as having counted her days of captivity back there in Parthia, pining for what she had lost. How great was her amazement, therefore, when she saw that far from dismissing Pazi's ridiculous question with the "Of course!" it deserved, Rachel seemed to be actually considering the question, and giving it great thought. And it was then that Chana and her brother, who had joined them in the meanwhile, heard for the first time about the *gosan,* an outlandish creature who appeared to be some kind of wandering minstrel, and about the song that had set Rachel wondering.

"I don't really remember all the words," Rachel said, "but it was something about a prince of Hyrcania - which Uncle Eliezer says is in fact the Gurgan Valley - whose parents had sent him to Babylonia - or was it Egypt? - for the pearl that was 'in the heart of the seas.' I never heard the end of the song, so I don't know if he ever found it, though I do remember that he set off on his journey and passed through many lands. But that doesn't matter. What really interested me was: what exactly was this pearl? My sister, Shirin, asked people in the village and they told her that it was a kind of gem that -"

"Yes, yes," Pazi said impatiently, "we all know what pearls are."

"But somehow I knew that it wasn't that kind of pearl the *gosan* was talking about. Then I told my . . . my brother, Issur, that I thought it wasn't something real at all, nothing that you could see or touch, but rather something inside of us; something that we had to find by ourselves. And so the word "Babylonia" kind of took root in me as the place I had to be in to find it, although Issur said that he didn't understand why it meant having to leave Parthia."

"And you were absolutely right," Chana said energetically, caught up in the discussion despite herself, and confident that she knew the answer to Rachel's conundrum. "You did have to come away to find it. The pearl is Judaism and the prince was sent to Egypt in search of it, just as the Israelites had been sent to Egypt so that Moses, four hundred years later, could receive the Torah there!"

Pazi's eyes grew wide. "And maybe," she said in an awed kind of voice, getting into the spirit of things, "maybe it was even *more* than that, Rachel: maybe it was the prayer that your very own father, may he rest in peace, instituted for the *havdalah* prayer at the end of the Sabbath - you know, the one that divides the sacred from the secular. For I have heard the rabbis say that 'Samuel instituted a pearl for us in Babylonia' - there you see? *Babylonia* - and I'm *sure* that they were referring to his prayer for the *havdalah*!"

Pazi looked triumphantly around the room to see the effect of her interpretation on the others. Chana, to her considerable pride, appeared very much struck by her words; and if backs were anything to go by, so was Tavi, over there by the stove, or at least so it seemed to Pazi. Rabbi Strabo also looked rather impressed, if not totally convinced. But Rachel just shook her head, unconsciously repeating the same gesture she had used that rainy spring morning so many years ago now, when discussing the very same subject with Issur and Shirin.

"No," she said firmly, though perhaps not quite as firmly as she had said it back then to Issur, for now that she was actually here in this Babylonia, the Babylonia of which the *gosan* had sung, nothing seemed quite as black and white as it had that long ago morning in Parthia. "No," she repeated, "I still think it isn't something so . . . so definable. I still think it's something inside of us, or that should be inside of us, and it's the 'how do we find it?' that bothered me then, and that's bothering me still."

Looking back at this conversation (and what in the world came over me, Chana wondered to herself, that I should start dealing in parables?), there was only one thing that emerged beyond any doubt whatsoever, and that was that Rachel needed to marry Rami, and to do it soon. Marriage with Huna's son would not only restore Rachel to her rightful place in society but also make her forget all these odd notions. Thus, in the wake of this conversation, Chana became more determined than ever to carry out Samuel's plans and to see that Rachel married Huna's son - and sooner rather than later. And for this reason, she set into motion the steps by which this marriage could be brought about.

Chapter Ten

The battle for Rachel's betrothal to Rami, the son of Rabbi Huna, began quietly enough. In the case which Chana soon brought to court over Rachel's inheritance, neither Chana nor Rabbi Nachman so much as mentioned the word "betrothal" or acted as if anything other than property was at stake: the property which belonged to Rachel as her share in her father's estate. To hear them speak, it was all a matter of houses and fields, rents and incomes. But even so, everyone knew that battle had been joined in the great marriage question, and the town followed the proceedings with interest.

The case was complex, to say the least. When Samuel died he left the guardianship of his two young daughters, and of the child his wife was expecting, to his close friend and confidant, Rabbi Joshua. Only, the times had been perilous and Samuel's careful plans had been overturned by the invasion of Nehardea and the subsequent death of both his wife and the intended guardian of his daughters. Now, Samuel was a wealthy man, for his father, Abba ben Abba, had been one of the leading silk merchants of Nehardea, and the caravans he sent every year to China yielded rich rewards. Samuel, moreover, had been a careful land-owner; some even said a miserly one, examining his broad acres in person and making sure that his property was properly maintained by the tenants who rented his fields and houses. And his efforts had been rewarded; on one occasion, as Samuel enjoyed repeating to whoever would listen, his daily rounds had allowed him to stop a rivulet that threatened to engulf his fields, and saved him who knows how many hundreds of *zuzim*. But all these riches were laid waste with the destruction of Nehardea, and by the time his two eldest daughters were redeemed from their short captivity, the little that was left from the wreckage of Samuel's property was turned into ready money for the benefit of the husbands whom they soon married in the Land of Israel. No one knew what had happened to Rachel, the child her father had not lived to see, and her share of the inheritance – should she still be alive or ever found – was put into the guardianship of first one sage and then another until, as the years passed, it ended up in the hands of Rabbi Isaac. Now, this Rabbi Isaac was a friend and colleague of Rabbi Nachman himself.

The question of Rachel's inheritance was thus a complicated one, and the sages of Nehardea attacked the case with gusto. Much of Rachel's inheritance had been sold or transferred by the various guardians, not always to her benefit; could such transactions be considered valid? Some said "no" and cited precedents to prove their point, and these were accused of favoring Chana; others said "yes" and cited precedents of their own, and these were accused of favoring Rabbi Nachman; still others were undecided, and these were accused of being ignorant. Then someone came up with a statement by the great Rabbi Simon ben Gamliel, may he rest in peace, saying that the guardian – in this case Rabbi Isaac - had to render an account of his guardianship to the Court, but here the Court – that is, Rabbi Nachman – disagreed, citing none other than Samuel himself, and the accusations began all over again. And then came the question of whether orphans, when they reached their majority, could contest the guardian's handling of their property, and on this point, everyone recalled that Samuel himself, may he rest in peace, thought that orphans could do so indeed, but here Rabbi Nachman disagreed with Samuel, saying "If so, then where is the Court's authority?" Soon everybody in Nehardea had the latest points of law at his or her fingertips, and housewives in the market place, and butchers at their blocks, and blacksmiths hammering away at their anvils, were all able to discuss every twist of the case down to the smallest detail. And everyone had an opinion.

* * *

This was not a pleasant time for Rachel. Though she knew very few details – and indeed she probably knew less than anyone else in Nehardea - she did know that people were talking about her and that the young girls with whom she mingled on Sabbath after synagogue, or with whom she chatted at the well at sunset, were looking at her with curious eyes and secret glances. She knew that Rabbi Huna was due to arrive in Nehardea soon, to look over his son's prospective bride and, perhaps, to come to terms with her aunt. And suddenly her adventures began to pall. She missed the wooded valleys of her homeland and the people she had known all her life. She wondered that she could ever have felt like an outsider in Parthia, or failed to realize what Shirin and Issur meant to her. For here in Nehardea she felt lonelier than ever. Here no one stopped to listen to her, or cared enough to ask "what are you thinking?" or to bring her into the group when the girls gathered together to talk. Apart from Rabbi Strabo, whose interest seemed to be purely scholarly, no one here was the least bit interested about her life back in the Gurgan Valley or about the family she had left behind. They had welcomed her back - and then forgotten her. It was as though her life in Parthia had never existed, or was a subject better avoided and best forgotten. Preparations for a holiday called Passover had begun, and they confused the girl and bewildered her. And now they were trying to marry her off. She began to wish she had never come.

One evening shortly after sunset, she stole out of the house and went for a walk along the river, brooding moodily over her thoughts and the events of recent weeks. But as she walked on her thoughts glided into dreams, and suddenly she was dreaming that she was back in Parthia; back at home with her family. She saw herself walking through thickly-branched forests of oak and elm, and Mother standing in front of the house, waving to her as she came home across the fields, and days, endless days, with Shirin and Issur. She remembered the horses cantering round the pastures in front of the house, neighing and snorting, manes streaming in the breeze, and the smell of the barns and the hay. She remembered the wild burst of color in the meadows at springtime and the bleating of the sheep as she folded them in for the night. She thought of that song - the *gosan*'s song - and wondered that it had ever disturbed her sleep; what pearl was there in Babylonia? She even thought about Rodoba, and smiled to think that she could ever have thought her disagreeable - Miriam outdid her by far!

Full of these pleasant visions she walked on and on, scarcely noticing that night had fallen and that the sounds of Nehardea were growing fainter and fainter as she left the city behind her. The waves lapped rhythmically against the river bank, at first softly but then with growing vigor as they forced themselves into her consciousness, awakening her with a start to the fact that she was here in Babylonia and not in Parthia at all. And then something - perhaps a bump in the ground, perhaps an innate sense of justice - caused the trend of her thoughts to shift, and she was forced to remember that she had not always been happy in Parthia. She began recalling all the times that she had felt so lonely and out of place there. All the times that she had stood on the sidelines, watching as the other girls enjoyed themselves and comforting herself with the thought that in another place, everything would be different. That if only she were in her rightful place, the place she was meant to be, she, Rachel, would have been a different person, not shy and timid as she was here in the Gurgan Valley, but light, gay, self-confident. Like Shirin, for example - or like the little girl she was sure she had once been, back in that other place, the place she'd been born.

But now she was back in that "other place," the city of her birth, and somehow things were not that different at all. True, her surroundings were different – indeed very different - but apart from that little had changed. She was still silent and shy; still puzzled by the things that brought joy to the people around her; still haunted by that sense of being alone and out of place. In her mind's eye she saw herself in the courtyard before the synagogue, talking with the other girls about this and that and stumbling over an unfamiliar word and amusing them with her accent and her ignorance; or at home with her aunt and uncle, wondering what in the world this thing called Passover - this strange holiday that was turning the entire household upside down - had to do with her; or wincing under Tavi's sharp tongue. She upbraided herself for not having tried harder in Parthia; surely it had all been her fault for not having felt more at home there, for having felt like such a misfit despite the love of her family. Surely it had only been that dream of some "other place" that had kept her from making the necessary efforts to fit in.

Only . . . a little voice inside of her asked whether she were not, in fact, making the very same mistake here in Nehardea, turning Parthia into that "other place" where everything would be alright, if only she could be there. Surely if she were back in Parthia she would miss Chana and her uncle and so many of the things that had become a part of her life here. Thus her thoughts swung back and forth and she was left feeling more confused and uncertain than ever: Nehardea, Parthia; Parthia, Nehardea. Where *did* she belong?

And then a new thought came to her, one that stopped her abruptly in her tracks: maybe she didn't really belong anywhere. Not in Parthia, and not in Babylonia. Maybe people didn't necessarily belong to one particular spot on earth. *Did* everything in the universe have its appointed place? *Was* there a divine scheme behind it all? In Parthia she had been taught to believe that there was, and here in Nehardea people seemed to have the same opinion; she couldn't help smiling as she recalled a certain dialogue between Chana and Tavi on this very subject not too long ago, Tavi solemnly declaring: "No one scratches even the tip of his finger unless Heaven wills it so," and Chana pointedly answering, "True; but the sages also say that everything comes from Heaven except cold drafts," at which Tavi had blushed and got up to close the kitchen door. Nevertheless, she herself wasn't so sure about this question of divine schemes. She herself had been violently uprooted as a child from her home in Nehardea. Only, maybe violent upheavals were part of the divine scheme, too. In Parthia she had seen towering oaks uprooted by storms, tossed on the forest floor like so many twigs. What was she but a twig herself, now snapped off, now grafted on?

She continued to walk along the river, listening to the waves of the Euphrates lapping steadily against the shore. It was dark and lonely. The moon had not yet risen, and she had never felt more desolate and alone in her life. From across the desert she could hear the wail of hyenas and the calls of the shepherds gathering their flocks for the night. She knew that Chana would be worried and that she should turn back home, but she continued walking nevertheless, feeling more and more anxious with every step, and less and less able to cope with this new life of hers now. Would it be possible, she wondered, to join a caravan and go back to Parthia? Perhaps one of the caravans on their way to India or China would accept a young woman willing to work for her passage. Or should she try to find a barge setting out for the cities along the upper Tigris, and make her way back from there? Overhead, the stars began to come out one by one, lighting up like little candles against the black sky.

"Like a garment inlaid with stars, that Ohrmazd puts on," she murmured to herself, recalling a fragment from one of the priest's hymns back home in Parthia. The words conjured up a host of memories, and feeling lonelier than ever she fell down on her knees before the swiftly flowing river.

"O Hordad," she prayed, "O great goddess of the sacred waters, hear my plea. You that are showered down, and you that stand in pools and vats. You that flow in the swift-moving rivers and you that swell the boiling seas: hear my prayer and help me. Help me to find my way back home."

She remained kneeling, lost in thought and unsure of what to do. She felt like walking on and on, and never returning to Nehardea at all. Finally, however, she rose to her feet and continued to walk along the river bank, trailing her fingers through the soft bull-rushes along the way. A wind had risen from across the desert and she was beginning to feel cold. She stopped again to consider what to do, when suddenly, someone bumped into her in the darkness and nearly knocked her off her feet. It was a man, and as she stumbled to catch her balance he grasped her by the arms in order to steady her. Startled, she turned to flee.

"Wait," the man said, removing his grip. "Don't go." His voice was gentle. She stopped and looked at him, straining to see his features in the darkness.

"Who are you?" he asked. "And what are you doing out by yourself at this hour?"

Rachel didn't answer, and they continued to gaze at each other. Slowly the darkness gave way and Rachel was able to make out the features of a handsome young man with black hair and white skin, slender and tall as . . . as the young birch trees that grew in the forests of Parthia. He seemed young; not too much older than herself. He looked at her curiously, knitting his brows in the effort to see who she was.

"You're not from Nehardea," he said at last. "But you really shouldn't be out here alone. Who are you visiting? They must be worried."

"I'm not afraid," Rachel replied, tossing her head. She resumed her walk along the river bank and the young man walked alongside her, glancing with amusement at her defiant expression.

"Why not?" he teased her. "How do you know I'm not from Nehar Peqoda?"

"Well, what if you are?" Rachel asked.

The young man smiled. "You must really come from far away. Around here there's a saying: 'If a Nehar Peqodan accompanies you, it's because of the fine cloak he saw on you.'"

Rachel laughed, and stopped in her tracks. "Do they really?"

Encouraged, the young man went on. "They do indeed. They also say, 'if a Pumbeditan accompanies you - change your accommodations!'"

"What else do they say?" Rachel asked curiously.

The young man paused, and looked at the young girl in front of him. "Well," he said slowly, "they also say, 'If a Nareshan kisses you, count your teeth!'"

They looked at each other, and for just a moment moved involuntarily towards each other in the darkness. Then the young man moved slightly away.

"And are you from Naresh?" Rachel asked lightly.

"No," he answered, "I'm from Sura. I'm here with my parents for the Passover, and also to attend to some business with my father." They continued walking in silence.

Rachel was still mulling over his previous words. For some reason, they upset her, and she tried to understand why. "But aren't they all Jews?" she asked finally. "I mean, the people from Nehar Peqoda, and from Naresh and from Pumbedita?"

"Yes, of course," the young man replied, somewhat started by her question. "But why do you ask?"

"They're all Jews, and yet that's the way they talk about each other?"

"Oh," he said, beginning to see what was bothering her. "Yes, they're all Jews - that is, they all pray to the same God and keep the same holidays. But that doesn't mean that they always like each other, or agree about everything. Or even that they are always kind to each other."

"No," Rachel said with some bitterness, remembering the glances that had been turned her way lately, and the unkind whispers from so many of her neighbors. "They aren't always kind to each other." They continued to walk along the river bank.

"But is it any different where you come from?" he asked her quietly, breaking the silence.

Rachel thought this over. No, it hadn't been any different there, either. A host of memories came rushing back: the teasing of some, the laughter of others, the cruel remarks out of jealousy or sheer unkindness. Only then, Shirin and Issur had always been on hand to defend her. Shirin might have bullied her at times, it was true, but only in the way that any older sister might have done, and she had always been quick to defend Rachel's place amongst the other girls in the valley. She thought of Shirin and Issur, and a wave of gratitude washed over her, and shame. How close she had come these past few months to forgetting them. And then, it was hard to feel self-righteous - was she any different herself? All those times when she had imagined herself better than the other girls in the valley, when she had scorned them in her heart, if not in actual words, for being silly, or ignorant, or just plain thoughtless. She realized now how wrong she had been to do so, and her heart ached with the realization. The young man walked at her side quietly, as though he was aware of the turbulence in her thoughts and unwilling to press her to talk.

"No," she admitted finally, and somewhat guiltily. "It's no different where I come from."

"Come to think of it, where *do* you come from?" he asked the girl, looking at her curiously.

"Parthia," she answered absently, still mulling over her own thoughts.

"Parthia!" he replied, startled. Then, "What is your name?"

She sighed. "Rachel."

"So you're Rachel!" the young man said thoughtfully.

"Yes, Rachel!" the girl said defensively. "Why not? Have you also -"

But before she could finish there was a loud rustle in the trees around them, and without warning people seemed to spring up out of nowhere.

"There she is!" Tavi declared, with obvious relief. Two burly men-servants from the house grabbed hold of the young man and held him firmly between them, while a third leveled a spear directly at his chest. Rabbi Strabo held up his lantern before the young man's face.

"Why, it's Huna's son!" he said in surprise. "Let go of him at once." The two servants, clearly disappointed at being balked of their prey, reluctantly let go of the young man. And in the midst of all the noise and confusion, everything suddenly became clear to Rachel.

"Rami?" she said, wonderingly. The two young people gazed long and earnestly at each other through the darkness. The trees formed a canopy over their head, and as Rachel gazed at him under the starlight she suddenly forgot that there was any other place in the world besides this.

"Come along," Tavi ordered abruptly, putting an end to the scene. "Let's get you home. The mistress is worried sick about you." And bundling the girl besides her, she took Rachel away and scolded her all the way back to Nehardea.

Chapter Eleven

Never had there been a spring like the one that blossomed that year during Passover. Everyone said so, and from the fields and synagogues praise for God's handiwork filled the skies. That year the grain fields seemed especially tender and golden, the date-palms greener and more fragrant than ever before. Broad fields of wheat and barley swayed proudly in the wind, and between them the grapes ripened on the vines.

For no one, perhaps, was the spring more beautiful than for Rachel. During the week of the Passover holiday Rami came every afternoon to fetch the girl from Chana's house and together they spent hours wandering through the fields and groves outside the ancient walls of the town. The rain was over and gone; the flowers had appeared on the earth and the voice of the turtle-dove was heard through the land. The Songs of Solomon, chanted in synagogue during the Passover holiday, came to life before their very eyes.

"In synagogue," Rami told her, "we are very careful how we touch the Scrolls of the Law. We wash our hands just so and never touch the parchment, but only point at the words with a silver pointer. But you: *ke-hut ha-shani siftotekh u-midbarekh naveh ke-felah ha-rimon* - your lips are like a thread of scarlet, and your forehead as beautiful as a piece of pomegranate."

"Oh!" Rachel breathed.

"I mean," Rami said quietly, "that you are the quintessence of all my dreams and hopes for a meaningful life." He paused for a few moments. "That is how it is."

Under other circumstances a young girl might not have been allowed to walk so freely with a young man who was not her betrothed - and perhaps not always even then - but with the question of Rachel's inheritance still in the balance, and the memory of Rachel's mother and Lajash still troubling her mind, Chana was too wise not to let Nature take things into her own capable hands. What could be better, she thought with satisfaction, than to have Rachel fall in love with Rami from the very beginning? That would keep her safe from any inappropriate love affairs - and in some way, perhaps, or so her heart whispered, make up for Shulamit's loss.

One afternoon towards the end of Passover, Rachel and Rami ventured further than usual into the countryside. They walked side by side in silence and Rachel found herself feeling unusually pensive, disturbed by whispers that had drifted back to her in synagogue that morning, from that part of the room where Yalta held sway. She knew that the holiday was almost over and that Rami would be returning to his fields near Sura before much longer. The wheat harvest would begin soon, and after that the planting of sesame and rice, and there was much for him to do there.

"I wonder," she said somewhat shyly, tentatively broaching a question that was troubling her, "whether you would still love me if I weren't - well, if I weren't me?"

Rami looked down at her in amusement. He was getting used to her questions, and always enjoyed teasing her. "But who would you be if you weren't you?" he asked her.

"Well," she replied, somewhat evasively, "Suppose I was just someone else and not Samuel's daughter at all? Suppose I was just the daughter of some Parthian farmer?"

"Well, well," Rami answered lightly, "that might be a problem!"

"Would it?" Rachel asked anxiously.

Rami stopped walking. He saw that she was really troubled, and he dropped his teasing tone. "That wouldn't be so terrible," he said gently. Didn't Joseph himself marry the daughter of an Egyptian?"

"He did?" Rachel said with relief, though not at the moment able to recall precisely who Joseph was.

"Yes, he did. Haven't the girls told you the story?" And he proceeded to tell Rachel about Joseph and Asenat, the daughter of Pentephres.

"They met in the first year of the seven years of plenty. Pharaoh sent Joseph to survey the whole land of Egypt and in the city of Heliopolis Joseph stayed with an Egyptian nobleman, a sun-worshipper named Pentephres. Now, this Pentephres had a daughter eighteen years old, as tall as Sarah and as beautiful as Rebecca. In fact," Rami said thoughtfully, "she might have been almost as beautiful as you."

Rachel blushed. She felt a happiness that was almost too much for her to bear. Rami continued his story.

"Now, just as Asenat was more beautiful than all the other girls, so was she more arrogant. She spurned the young men who sought her hand, and dressed in gold and in valuable ornaments, all of them carved with the names of the Egyptian gods. But when she saw Joseph for the first time, alighting from his chariot in front of her father's house, she was strongly cut to the heart, and her soul was crushed, and her knees and entire body trembled. And she fasted for a week, and prayed to Joseph's God to accept her and to marry her to Joseph."

Rachel listened, her heart racing. She felt as though she were Asenat herself. Had she not also been cut to the heart the first time she saw Rami? She remembered looking up at his face that first night in the darkness. Would God grant Asenat her wish? Would God grant her hers?

". . . and then Asenat led Joseph into her father's house. And Joseph said, 'Let one of the virgins come and wash my feet.' And Asenat said to him, 'No, my Lord, why should another come for that? Your feet are my feet, and your hands are my hands, and your soul is my soul.' Then they embraced each other for a long time and interlocked their hands like strong bonds that none can break apart." Rami paused in his recital.

Rachel took Rami's hand with both of hers, and held it tightly. It was the first time they had touched so. "Like that?" she asked him.

Rami looked straight back at her. "Like that," he replied softly.

Rachel clung to his hand for a few more moments, and then slowly let it go. "But did they marry?" she asked finally, almost afraid of the answer

"Yes, they married," Rami assured her, smiling. "Pharaoh himself put golden crowns on their heads and blessed them, saying 'May the Lord God the Most High bless you and multiply you and magnify and glorify you forever.'"

"And then what happened?" asked Rachel.

Rami paused. The story ended there, but Rachel was clearly expecting something more. So he did his best.

"Well," he said, floundering, "Asenat became a good Jewish wife, and gave up idol worship, and she and Joseph lived happily ever after in their palace in Pharaoh's city."

"She gave up her idols?" Rachel asked.

"Of course," Rami replied.

Rachel thought this over for a few moments, and then nodded her head in acquiescence. "Alright. But what about her family? Didn't she ever see them again?"

"No, of course not," said Rami grandly, getting into the spirit of things. "When she gave up her idols she said, 'Your gods are my gods, and your people are my people,' so of course there was no reason for her to ever see them again."

"Oh!" said Rachel. She was not entirely pleased by the end of the story; and in fact, it bothered her a great deal. Walking silently along she tried to analyze her feelings. What was it that made her so uneasy? It took her a few moments to translate her thoughts into words, but then she stopped and faced Rami in great earnest.

"But supposed she hadn't been the daughter of this – what was his name?"

"Pentephres," Rami supplied.

"Of this Pentephres, of this nobleman," she continued. "Suppose there was no golden crown, and no noble father – would Joseph still have married her?"

Rami looked at her, somewhat puzzled by the question, and even more by the note which he caught in Rachel's voice.

"But she *was* the daughter of a nobleman," he replied.

"But what if –"

"What if my grandmother had wheels?" he broke in shortly; he was getting tired of the whole conversation.

"She was who she was; there's no point in wondering about what ifs." And they turned back to Nehardea, and began to walk in the direction of the widow's house.

* * *

It was during one of these walks outside of the city-gates that Rabbi Huna's wife came to visit Chana, as it behooved her to do now that a marriage between the families seemed imminent. Now, Chova and Chana had known one another all their lives, having played together as girls in Huzul, the small farming village halfway between Sura and Nehardea where Chova grew up, and where Chana occasionally went to visit her mother's family. In days gone by Chana had ranked higher than Chova on the local social scale, for her father was learned and well-to-do, and while she had been married to Phineas, the son of the rich merchant Abba, Chova had had to make do with Huna, then just a poor student earning his keep by toiling out in the fields and the date groves of the rich farmers. Since then, however, much had changed, and now Chana was a widow of moderate means while Chova was the wife of the Chief Judge of Sura, the rich and renowned Rabbi Huna. Yet none of these factors had ever affected the relations between the two women, which had been cordial and friendly since childhood. Chova, painfully shy as a child and lacking in self-confidence, had remained shy and diffident even during these years of prosperity, and out of habit and temperament looked up to Chana as the stronger personality of the two. Thus a meeting between the two women prior to the official engagement should have been a pleasant task for both of them, and in sending his wife in the vanguard of negotiations, so to speak, Rabbi Huna indeed hoped to signal that his intentions were honorable – whatever might be decided in the end.

Unfortunately, however, the visit did not go quite as planned. Learning, somehow, of the upcoming visit, Yalta contrived to take part in it, too, by the simple expedient of running into Chova when Chova's foot was all but on Chana's doorstep. Thus it happened that when Tavi opened the door that afternoon, Chana found herself with not one but two guests on her hands, and one of them not particularly welcome. Yalta sailed into the atrium with her accustomed assurance, but Chova crept in after her, appalled at the turn of events, and through a series of mute but highly eloquent glances attempted to signal to her hostess that it was none of her doing. But Chana did not need to be told this. She took in the situation with a glance, greeted both guests with a look of friendly tranquility, and sent Tavi off to the kitchen in order to bring refreshments. Tavi went alertly enough, though not without first shooting a look of suspicion in Yalta's direction. She, too, knew Yalta of old.

"Where is Rachel?" Yalta asked Chana after the first greetings were over, though she knew perfectly well where Rachel was even without asking: not for nothing did she have good servants. Chana suspected as much but she answered her mildly nevertheless. "She's out walking with Rami," she said, and looked over at Chova, who smiled nervously.

Yalta, looking as disapproving as she could, which was very disapproving indeed, clicked her tongue and said, "O dear! What's to be done with the young people these days? We surely did not go gadding around with the rogues when *we* were girls."

"She's with *Rami*," protested Rami's mother, sitting up straight.

"To be sure," Yalta murmured, dismissing the matter with a conciliatory wave of the hand and turning her attention to the platter of fruit that Tavi was now offering the guests. The finest fruits of the season - plums, figs, thinly sliced melons - glistened in enticing array against the glass platter. Yalta chose a plum, and then biting into it, looked the fruit over rather disparagingly from all sides. "Ah," she said, "it *is* rather late in the season, of course," and set the fruit down. Chova hastily swallowed a bite from her own plum, hoping her enjoyment of it hadn't been too obvious, and Chana ostentatiously took two plums for herself and plunked them down on her plate. Chana made polite conversation with Yalta, in which the subject of the weather figured prominently.

Chova maintained a resentful silence. Mild though she was, that reference to Rami had greatly vexed her. But, then, all her conversations with Yalta had a way of going astray. She could still remember her first conversation with Yalta, back in the early days when she, Chova, was a newly married bride, easily flustered and painfully shy, and Yalta an established matron of position and wealth. Now, it so happened that Yalta, in those days, affected a hairstyle quite unlike that worn by any other Jewish matron in Nehardea, or indeed anywhere else in the Euphrates Valley. And no sooner did Chova see that elaborately coifed and braided head than she exclaimed, "Oh! It's just like the Empress's!" Not that Chova had much to do with empresses, of course, but once, on a visit to relatives in Ctesphion across the river, she had seen the marble bust of a woman with just such a hairstyle as Yalta - a souvenir from the last Roman "visit" to that oft-beleaguered city - and upon inquiring had been told: "That? That's the Empress of Rome!" Now, Chova had meant nothing that wasn't complimentary, but Yalta had only sniffed at her comment, as though to say: "Who is this empress that she should look like me?" And from that moment, Chova knew that her relations with Yalta would never be good. Thus, it had been with extreme trepidation that she heard of the engagement between her son Rami, and Yalta's daughter, Doneg. Not that Chova had anything against the girl herself, whom she occasionally saw on her infrequent visits to Nehardea, walking in the market-place with her friends or trailing after her mother on the way home from synagogue.

"I suppose you'll be sending Rachel off to her sisters before long," said Yalta, though in truth she supposed no such thing.

"Well," said Chana, "perhaps after the marriage. For a wedding trip, you know. Rachel is naturally eager to see them but I think it best that she remain here for a while. After all, there is so much for her to get used to."

"So I hear," Yalta murmured.

Chana flushed; she had fallen into *that* trap without even realizing it. But Chova, still angry with Yalta, came unexpectedly to the rescue.

"I saw Rachel a few weeks ago in the market place with her uncle - it was just a glimpse - but she's lovely, Chana, and so like her mother. It must give you a lot of pleasure to have her back with you. Almost like old times, before all the troubles." Chana nodded, her cheeks flushing slightly, almost shyly, at the reference to days of old. So much had changed.

"Yes," conceded Yalta. "She is very lovely. And so fortunate that she doesn't take after her dear father! After all," she continued, glancing over at Chova, "one never knows *what* will come down in the family," and looked so expressive that Chana and Chova both had a sudden image of Samuel in all the glory of his bad teeth and big stomach. Chova looked decidedly alarmed.

"Quite true," agreed Chana. "One never knows with these things. How fortunate that Doneg has turned out so well!"

"Yes, indeed!" agreed Chova, and then turned pale. There was no telling how Yalta would interpret *that* remark. Fortunately, however, Tavi entered the room just then, this time bearing a tray of cakes, and armed neutrality reigned once again. Yalta shook her head at the cakes, as though finding fault with them, and stood up to go. Chova was anxious for a few private words with Chana and showed a tendency to linger, but Yalta, on guard against insurrection, soon put an end to that. "What a shame," she said, "that we have to go now. But we surely don't wish to overstay our welcome!" at which Chova was obliged to rise, too, and make her farewells. And thus Rabbi Huna's good-will embassy came to an end. Tavi, who had heard every word that was spoken (and many that were not), was fuming. It was all very well for *her* to find fault with Rachel – that was her privilege and duty! - but Rachel was Samuel's daughter, and it wasn't for other folks – namely Yalta - to find fault as well. And she slammed the door after them.

Later that evening, Chana found an opportunity to tell Eliezer about Yalta's visit, which she did with wry humor and considerable detail, right down to the interlude with the plums. "And this is the woman," Chana concluded, winding up her story, "whose own husband has said: 'Arrogance is not becoming to women.' I heard him say it with my own ears!"

"Oh, Yalta knows everything," Eliezer returned mildly. "I once heard Benjamin the Shepherd telling Hisda some problems he was having around lambing time, when Nachman walked by, and overhearing the conversation he told Benjamin just what to do: 'When the ewe kneels for lambing,' he said, 'place one oily compress on her forehead and one on her womb, to keep her warm. That's the best course of all - you can take it from Yalta!'"

At which Chana just shook her head, and laughed a bit ruefully. Take it from Yalta indeed.

* * *

Two days after the visit to Rachel's aunt, which was not repeated, Rami and his parents returned to Sura. The date for the wedding ceremony was tentatively set for Hanukkah some eight months away, and Chana set vigorously to work. By then, she reasoned, ticking off the list of things yet to settle, Rachel's inheritance would be secure and Rabbi Huna ready to sign the marriage contract.

But Rachel had been more upset than she realized by that last conversation with Rami, and deep inside herself she began to brood.

Chapter Twelve

Spring ripened into summer, and summer into fall. The Days of Awe came and went, and then the Feast of Tabernacles, and in the synagogues they began to recite the prayers for rain, as they did every year at that time. Only this year the rains did not fall and the dog-days of summer dragged on. The fields were beginning to look parched, and the newly pruned vines, only recently relieved of their rich black grapes, began to shrivel and dry in the vineyards. If things continued like this much longer, the freshly sown crops of barley and wheat would wither in the ground before they even had a chance to sprout. Farmers and housewives alike began to look worried. Here and there, some people even whispered the dreaded word "drought."

Out in the market place and the Houses of Study, old men reminisced over earlier periods of drought and regaled the young with their stories. Why, the last drought hadn't been so bad, one old man tried to comfort the young people. The rains had come late - yes, just like this year - and wheat had grown scarce and hard to come by. Some of the richer householders had even sold their fine mansions in exchange for wheat! But no harm in that. Rabbi Nachman had just made the speculators give the houses back once the barges rounded the river and the city received its supplies again. And after that, of course, the rains finally came.

"Yes," said another, "but what about the time the pestilence came together with the drought?"

"Or," broke in another old man, shaking his head, "the time that wolves devoured two children across the Euphrates? The drought caused a bad famine that year."

Yes, those had been bad times indeed. People clucked their tongue and continued to look anxiously up at the heavens.

* * *

Rachel worried about Rami. She had not seen him since the end of the Feast of Tabernacles, when he had returned to Sura. Had the drought struck there too? Nightly she looked for Tishtrya, the star that carried the seeds of all waters. Tishtrya would bring the rains. When no one was looking, she went down to the river and murmured the hymns she remembered from home, back in Parthia:

"We sacrifice unto Tishtrya, the bright and glorious star, for whom the flocks and the herds and the farmers all long. When shall we see him rise up, the bright and glorious star Tishtrya? When will the springs run with waves as thick as a horse's girth, and still thicker?"

Rachel paused and looked cautiously around to make sure she was alone. She was, and so she continued.

"We sacrifice unto Tishtrya, the bright and glorious star, for whom long the standing waters, and the running spring-waters, the stream-waters and the rain-waters. When will the bright and glorious Tishtrya rise up for us? When will the springs -"

Rachel became suddenly aware that someone was watching her. She rose guiltily to her feet and saw to her dismay that it was Miriam; she of the silken tunics and the nasty temper. Rachel was never glad to see her at any time, but she was particularly dismayed just now, apprehensive lest Miriam had overheard her speaking. What a scandal Miriam would make: Samuel's daughter offering prayers to Parthian rain goddesses!

"Reciting psalms?" Miriam inquired knowingly, with all the condescension of a newly-married woman to a girl whose wedding was still months away. Rachel nodded, relieved, to be sure, at Miriam's interpretation of her actions, but her teeth on edge nevertheless. There was something in Miriam's tone that always made her blood rise.

"Well," Miriam told her, "there's no need for you to do that. There's still time for the rains to come, and they may come yet. But if there is a real drought, the rabbis will declare a *ta^canit* and then we'll all be out in the market place saying our prayers day and night. So it's best to wait."

"What is a *ta^canit*?" Rachel asked curiously.

"Oh!" Miriam exclaimed with feigned surprise, smoothing the folds of her cloak with a graceful hand, "I forgot that you don't know very much. You see, if the rains don't come, it's because of our sins. Everything is because of our sins, of course, but the rains especially. So if it's a drought, the rabbis will declare a fast and then everyone will gather out in the market place underneath the open sky and pray till God forgives us and it starts to rain. That's a *ta^canit*."

Now, if it had been anyone else, Rachel would have listened with interest, anxious to learn anything she knew Rami believed. His god was her god, and his ways her ways too. But this Miriam had a way of talking down to her, and Rachel would have liked nothing better than to shock the girl out of her self-complacency.

"Oh, is that why the droughts come?" Rachel asked, politely dubious. "At home, they always told us that it was because Tishtrya, the goddess of rain, had been worsted in battle by Apaosha, the Drought-Demon. Apaosha, you see, takes the form of an ugly black stallion and they fight hoof to hoof, and then -"

Miriam interrupted her here, brushing away Rachel's childhood and several thousand years of Parthian beliefs with a disdainful wave of her hand. "It's because of our sins," she said firmly. And with that, the girls turned and walked back to town. No, there was no shocking Miriam.

* * *

In the meantime, the case over Rachel's inheritance dragged on. The month of *Tishrei* saw the courts closed for the High Holidays, and busy though Chana was in preparing first for the Jewish New Year, and then for the Day of Repentance, and finally, for the week-long Feast of Tabernacles, all of which crowded each other in endless succession, she grew more and more impatient of the delay. But even *Tishrei* eventually comes to an end, and one day soon after the Feast of Tabernacles, court re-convened and the question of a large field pertaining to Rachel's inheritance appeared on the first day's agenda. Rachel had inherited this field from her father, of course, but it had passed through a great many hands during those years of her absence and was now the subject of no little contention. Nevertheless, Chana had high hopes for the outcome; she knew that Rabbi Judah, the Chief Judge of Pumbedita, would be attending court that day, and Rabbi Judah had been one of Samuel's most respected colleagues.

But before the question of Rachel's field could be broached, there were other, more immediate matters to deal with. Like every year around harvest time, disputes had arisen between landowners and farmhands, and these had to be resolved first of all. The first case, therefore, involved a hired laborer who claimed one half of the field he had harvested, while the field's owner contended that they had agreed to only one third of the profit. Neither side could produce a written contract, so Nachman ruled: "The owner is believed," and turned to the next case.

But Rabbi Judah stood up and disagreed. "Surely it all depends on local usage?" he asked, in a dry tone of voice. And then both he and Rabbi Nachman said at one and the same time, "Samuel says" - and broke off their sentence in confusion, and looked at each other askance.

Rabbi Judah was the first to recover. "Samuel always said that in such a case, where there is no contract, it all depends on local usage."

But Rabbi Nachman shook his head. "Surely my respected colleague from Pumbedita is mistaken;" he said politely; Rabbi Judah, after all, was a visitor. "Samuel always said that the owner is to be believed," he remarked amiably, and with that seemed to consider the case closed.

But Rabbi Judah continued to object, and the two of them wrangled on till Nachman resolved the issue by simply moving on to the next case. It was, after all, his courtroom.

The next case dealt with the question of how much ground should be left between vineyards and date-trees; a perennial problem that was somehow never quite resolved from one year to the next. Rabbi Joseph, it seemed, owned some date-trees adjoining a vineyard owned by Rabbi Hanan, and the latter declared that the birds roosting in Joseph's trees swooped down and damaged his vines, and that the trees should therefore be cut down.

But Joseph strenuously objected to this, pointing out that he had left four cubits between his trees and the vines, as required by law. "And I am not going to cut down a tree that gives a *kab* of dates every year. You, sir, can cut it down if you like." And with that he sat back down.

Rabbi Judah stood up. "Rabbi Joseph is correct," he stated. "Samuel himself ruled that between four and eight cubits must be left between the trees and the vines." And he sat back down, as though the last word had been said.

But Nachman shook his head. "Indeed, sir," he said politely, "you are mistaken" - and with an effort bit back the words "yet again". "Samuel said that eight to sixteen cubits should be left."

There was a buzz of voices in the courtroom, some agreeing with Rabbi Hanan and Rabbi Nachman, others agreeing with Rabbi Joseph and Rabbi Judah. But Rabbi Ammi, in the second row, was disgusted by the whole thing. "All this fuss over what Samuel says," he said, whispering bitterly to his neighbor. "Everyone knows that Samuel only looked out for himself." Now, Rabbi Ammi had made similar comments on other occasions, and this one might have gone ignored as usual, but Rabbi Judah's presence in court that day made Nachman unusually sensitive to criticism, and when he saw the scholars in the second row whispering he turned purple with rage. "What are you saying back there?" he thundered.

Rabbi Ammi stood up and repeated his comment. Nachman, glad to find a vent for his anger since Rabbi Judah was off-limits, snapped out, "You dare to criticize Samuel?!"

And again Rabbi Ammi stood up and shouted back, "Yes, I dare! Why not? Everyone knows it's true. Samuel only looked out for himself. Look what happened in Caesarea-Mazaca. The Jews there were slaughtered by King Shapur, but did Samuel ever protest? Oh, no, of course not; Samuel was too busy being Shapur's buddy to even rend his garments as a sign of mourning."

There was another buzz in the courtroom. Everyone knew the incident to which Rabbi Ammi referred, and faces were troubled and perplexed. Rabbi Isaac spoke up a bit timidly and said, "But, Ammi, you know that King Shapur himself said that he never put a single Jew to death."

"No?" Ammi sneered back. "I suppose it was the harp-strings of the Jews that burst the walls of the city, like the trumpets at Jericho, and allowed Shapur's soldiers to enter and slaughter them all." Rabbi Ammi was white with rage, and shaking in anger. His own father had come from eastern Anatolia, not far from the great city of Caesarea-Mazaca, and Ammi had heard the whole story from his own lips.

The room was silent. No one else really believed that Samuel had turned his back on the Jews of Caesarea-Mazaca, or that such a massacre had even taken place. But there were more than a few in that courtroom who could remember instances when Samuel's rulings had gone counter to their own interests, and rather perilously close to his own. Rabbi Zutra stood up. "I remember the time," he said slowly, "that Samuel ordered me to reimburse the owner of an oil factory when I broke some jars that were standing where they had no business to be."

Rabbi Judah stood up, ready to argue. "And what's wrong with that?" he inquired. "We've done the same in Pumbedita."

And Rabbi Zutra replied, "Yes, but later I learned that Samuel had an interest in that factory." There was a long silence, and then a growing clamor of voices until almost all of the sages there were dredging up old grievances, and not only with Samuel but with one and other as well, many of which went back to the first terrible days following the destruction of Nehardea. Anger at perceived injustices during those first terrible years when the wealth of the city lay in ashes, wrath at unfair advantages and methods in the ensuing reconstruction, burst forth in the courtroom, all the more violent for having festered in silence all these long years. Voices became more and more acrimonious, and Rabbi Nachman had to rap on the table for silence more than once.

"That's enough," he said. "That's enough. We have other cases to hear today." And after a short silence, during which no one looked at his neighbor, he turned to the question of Rachel's field.

Later that evening, Eliezer reported back to Chana and gave a full account of that day in court, without omitting a single detail. "In short," he said, winding up his report, "the case is still undecided. It's hard to say, but Nachman may get his way after all and leave Rachel's fields in other hands."

"But Rabbi Judah disagrees with Nachman," Chana pointed out. "He told us so himself."

"Yes," Eliezer replied pleasantly, "but Rabbi Judah always disagrees with everyone."

"Humph," was all that Chana said in reply to this, but in her heart she knew her brother was right. Rabbi Judah never did agree with anyone. He was an uncomfortable ally, and perhaps even a dangerous one. Chana sighed, and changed the subject.

The case over Rachel's field resumed the next day, but nothing in court was quite as it should be. Tempers were short and recriminations were frequent, often on issues that were completely tangential to the matter at hand. That bitter discussion the day before had reopened old wounds, and as the days went by the community became more and more agitated, and more deeply divided than ever before.

* * *

In the middle of all this, royal horsemen galloped into Nehardea to proclaim the news that was rapidly spreading across the broad lands of the Persian Empire: Shapur, the King of Kings, was dead. From the Oxus to the Euphrates, people huddled in groups to discuss the momentous tidings. Many were those who could remember no king but Shapur, and his great deeds and victories had become legendary in his own time. This was a king who had taken the Roman emperor captive with his own hands! Would Prince Hormizd measure up to his father?

Nehardea greeted the news with interest and even relief, for it gave people something new to talk about; and in these days, when old grievances and predictions of drought were on everyone's lips, the change of topic was welcome indeed. In Chana's house, however, no one had any thought for either the change of regime or the ominous lack of rain. Instead, all was bustle and commotion for the wedding of Rachel and Rami, which Chana now felt confident was soon to take place. Rachel's inheritance was shaping up nicely, Chana thought, and surely it wouldn't be long before she and Rabbi Huna came to terms over the matter. Thus Chana scarcely had time to think about the death of King Shapur or about anything else. There was so much to do and prepare!

"Now, Tavi," Chana asked her housekeeper, "How many sheets will Rachel be taking with her? We have to make sure that they are of the finest linen - from Pumbedita if at all possible, and from Borsippa if not. None of that coarse stuff the maid brought home from market last week; *that* was about as soft as a Rodian sack."

"Yes, ma'm," Tavi replied, through a mouthful of pins, as she cut through a bolt of fine linen that would make a new *chiton* for the young bride. Rachel stood patiently as one of the maids pinned the material around her. Suddenly, she spied through the open window a group of young girls hurrying off in the direction of the market place.

"Oh, Aunt," she cried. "Can't I go with them? I want to see what all the commotion's about." Tavi started to grumble, but Chana waved her off with a smile.

In a minute Rachel was out of the house, on her way to catch up with her friends. She walked as quickly as she could - Rachel knew that it would never do for an almost married woman to run, and these days she was as obedient as even Chana could wish. The streets were filled with a fine yellow dust and the sun burned down hot and relentless. She turned the corner near the market-place, when to her surprise she found her way blocked by a fierce-looking warrior on a richly mounted horse. She craned her neck upwards to see what could be the meaning of this obstacle. As her eyes got used to the dazzling sunlight, she took in the soldier's bronzed face and powerful arms, tanned and bared to the sun, and suddenly she let out a gasp.

"Issur!" she exclaimed.

"Rachel!" the young soldier exclaimed back, jumping off his horse with a swift movement and tossing his reigns to the rider that came galloping up beside him. "I was just about to start asking for the house of Chana the Widow. I never thought it would be so easy to find you!" He unstrapped the helmet from his head and called out a few words to his comrades, who reigned in behind him, their horses pawing the ground with high-bred impatience. He seemed bigger than she remembered, and his hair was caught back in a leather string that emphasized the strongly modeled lines of his face and jaw.

Rachel stared at Issur, her first feeling of delight giving way to a tumult of emotion and fear. Here was a ghost, a figure from another life. Another life altogether. She forgot that just a few months ago she had been offering up fervent prayers to the river goddess, begging for help in returning home to Parthia as swiftly as possible. But those few months might have been centuries so far as Rachel was concerned now. What was Issur doing here?

"What *are* you doing here?" she asked uneasily.

"Why, I've come to get you," he grinned down at her. Rachel's eyes raced across his bronzed features, taking in his elegantly caparisoned horse and heavy military equipment. He noticed her glance and smiled sheepishly.

"Never could hide anything from you," he admitted, smiling. "I'm with the royal bodyguard in Ctesiphon, just over the river. We've come from Parthia to take part in the coronation of Prince Hormizd, the new King of Kings. After that, we'll be continuing on to Sogdiana with the King's army to subdue the tribes across the border. But on the way over I'll take you back home, just as I promised Mother and Shirin."

"Mother," Rachel said slowly. "How is she? And how is Shirin?"

"Mother's fine," Issur replied, puzzled by the hesitancy in her manner. "Shirin married Rustam last fall, of course, and they have settled into that empty farm further up the valley - you know the one I mean? The one that belonged to that uncle of his who died a few years ago." His eyes wandered over her, and took in the fine linen *chiton* and the silver and gold decorating her arms and throat. "You look beautiful, Rachel," he said quietly. "But different somehow."

"I'm getting married," Rachel replied desperately, almost without thinking.

"You're getting married?" Issur replied, completely bewildered. "And just who are you thinking of marrying, may I ask?"

"Rabbi Huna's son. You see, he was engaged to me, that is, you know, to Samuel's daughter, even before I was born," she replied, completely flustered.

Issur digested this slowly. "But you're Kovad's daughter," he pointed out reasonably. "So you don't have to marry anyone. Anyone but me, that is."

"But I want to," she explained desperately. "I love him, and he loves me too, and what does it matter anyway? You can have Rodoba, or Ardush-"

"Rachel!" Issur exploded. "I told Shirin you never should have come. This has gone on long enough. You're not this "Samuel's daughter," no matter who's engaged to marry her.

You are Rachel, the daughter of Kovad and a true daughter of Parthia. Your place is at home in Parthia, and the sooner I get you back there, the better."

The two stood silently, facing each other like enemies.

"When is this `marriage' supposed to take place?" he asked finally, breaking the silence between them.

"During *Maidhyairya*," Rachel replied, almost in a whisper, reverting back to Parthian reckoning of time without even realizing it. "That is, around Hanukkah time, six weeks from now." Issur flung himself back on his horse, and pulled in the reigns so sharply that the horse reared and tossed back its head. Rachel jumped away.

"I'll be back before then," Issur informed her sternly. "And I'm taking you back home where you belong, Rachel. This has gone on long enough."

Rachel watched him ride off in a swirl of yellow dust, standing alone in the quiet street as though rooted to the spot. For some reason, she suddenly felt more alone than she had ever felt in her life; crushingly, terrifyingly alone.

She stood staring long after he had gone, almost too numb to think, until she finally came to her senses and turned to go. Suddenly she saw Yalta standing next to one of the houses, smiling at her with a look of vindictive triumph. Without doubt, she had heard every word.

Chapter Thirteen

Yalta was very thorough. Within minutes of Rachel's brief conversation with Issur the whole town knew that Rachel had had a secret rendezvous with a heathen soldier, that the two of them had whispered together alone, and that Samuel was turning over in his grave. The interest in Rachel's court case, which had considerably flickered during the last few months, now flared up again and with ever greater strength. For Rabbi Nachman changed his tactics. Though previously content to fight Rachel in terms of property, he had no compunction in using a weapon which she herself had placed in his hands; so throwing caution to the winds he decided to broach the question of marriage head on. And thus he now embarked on the most delicate subject of all, the laws of ritual purity, drawing attention to that aspect of Rachel's captivity which had never as yet been mentioned in public. How? - he demanded - looking around the hushed court with an expression that was both righteous and outraged, how could Rachel be considered a fit bride for the son of Rabbi Huna? Who could guarantee her virginity? Had she not been a captive all these years? Why, Samuel himself, may he rest in peace, had never put any credit in the testimony of women taken captive by pagans, and who later declared that they had remained undefiled.

This, unfortunately, was all too true. Even Rachel's well-wishers - and there were many who secretly opposed the arrogant Nachman - were unable to deny this sad fact. One old man, who had been a friend of Samuel's father, shook his head sadly and recalled the time some Jewish women taken captive by the Palmyrians returned to Nehardea and declared themselves pure according to the strictest rabbinical criteria. Samuel's father, Abba the silk-merchant, had accepted their testimony and appointed guardians for the young women till they could be ransomed. But Samuel, young and zealous in the pursuit of the Law, questioned their testimony with the arrogance of youth.

"Who has guarded them until now?" he asked pointedly.

At this, Abba reproached his son and said: "And if these had been your own daughters, would you be so quick to judge?"

Alas, Abba's words had come to pass, and now it was Samuel's own daughter whose fate hung in the balance. But Chana and her supporters stood fast, reminding people that Rachel had, after all, been only four years old when taken captive, and that the laws of purity did not therefore apply. Chana quoted rabbinic authorities in favor of her position, Nachman quoted others in favor of his, and everyone had an opinion.

* * *

The weeks stretched out. The skies remained a dull copper color and the rains refused to fall. The rabbis had not yet declared a drought, but some of the town's leading householders fasted and prayed three times a week for the drought to end. It wouldn't be long, people whispered, before the rabbis would be blowing the *shofar*. And when the girls gathered around the well in the late afternoons, they too discussed the drought and what it would mean for the coming year. Rachel was appalled by the disasters they foretold so knowledgeably, repeating the gossip they overheard at home. As they talked they watched the flocks return from the pasture, filing down the street at the heels of the goat-herd, each goat turning obediently into its own yard as the line made its way through the town. Every now and then one of the girls would dart out to guide a hopeful goat that had mistaken a promising bit of herbage for its own, and giving it a push in the right direction, resumed her place among the chattering girls. One evening towards sunset, as Rachel came up to the girls at their usual gathering spot, she was just in time to overhear Miriam giving a spiteful account of their last conversation together. "And after *that*," Miriam continued, "she said, 'the Drought-Demon takes on the form of an ugly black stallion . . .'" and then stopped as one of the girls nudged her arm as Rachel approached. There was an awkward silence.

Hadas, the daughter of Rabbi Ashi, tried to give the conversation a different complexion. She turned to Rachel and said, "But don't worry, Rachel, no matter how bad the drought is, it shouldn't affect your wedding. Even if the drought isn't over by Hanukkah the ceremony will still take place."

"Assuming," Miriam broke in, "that everything concerning your . . . umm, your *inheritance* is settled by then." At this, some of the girls snickered. Others, however, gasped with dismay. The subject of Rachel's inheritance battle was strictly taboo, and had never so much as been mentioned in any of these market-place enclaves. And, now, here was Miriam hinting at a subject more delicate by far.

"We don't know that," Doneg declared, with a good deal of rebuke in her voice. She was responding solely to Miriam's spoken words; utterly refusing to snap at the bait which Miriam had dangled. The other girls admired Doneg for taking Rachel's part, for they knew, of course, that she had been formally betrothed to Rami, and there were some who thought that she was, in fact, actually in love with Rami, on the basis of certain glances they had overseen, or thought they had overseen, in synagogue. Yet for all this, Doneg had never once spoken against Rachel or jeered at what some people referred to as "Chana's pretensions," even when it was her own mother, as it frequently was, who led such remarks. But Doneg refused to stoop to such behavior. If Rami loved Rachel – and from what she heard it seemed that he did – then she, Doneg, was not going to stand between them. So she turned reprovingly to Miriam and the other girls who had snickered and said sharply, "Very likely it won't matter one way or the other just how much she inherits - Rabbi Huna surely had no need for more wealth."

Rachel flushed. She knew that Doneg was trying to be kind, but the entire subject filled her with shame. And not only shame, but fear. She had never quite forgotten that conversation with Rami and his complacency over Asenat's golden crowns, but now the memory washed over her and filled her with anxiety. Would marriage with Rami depend on the number of fields and groves the court eventually granted her? And now all these slurs, these dreadful slurs. Rami loved her – she was sure he loved her. But did he love her enough? Enough to marry her no matter what? The question pounded in her head till she was sure that all the other girls must hear it, too. Tears rose to her eyes, blinding her to the market-place around her, even as her home in Parthia, and Shirin and Issur, seemed to appear before her very eyes, and with such startling clarity that her heart contracted inside of her and filled with pain.

Chapter Fourteen

There was no longer any doubt. The first cold days of *Kislev* had come and gone, and there was still no rain in sight. This was a drought, all right. Oh, there had been one rainfall earlier that autumn, but that had been a gentle rain, good for the crops, perhaps, but not for the trees, and certainly not enough to fill the deep cataracts of the river. The fields turned brown and dry and people went around with their eyes turned towards Heaven. When would God hear their prayers?

In the synagogues, the leaders of the community fulfilled their duty and observed a series of fasts three days a week. But the skies remained cold and hard as iron, and in the market place people were beginning to grumble. Why, they asked pointedly, were their prayers going unanswered?

"Take Rabbi Hanina ben Dosa," one man said. "There he was, walking along the road one day and the rain started to fall. 'O Master of the Universe!' he called out. 'Why should I be in distress and the rest of the world at ease?' Immediately the rain stopped. When he reached home, he said, 'O Master of the Universe! why should I be at ease and the rest of the world in distress?' and immediately the rain fell once again."

Everyone sighed. Those were the days. They didn't make them like Rabbi Hanina any more.

Rabbi Kattina, a flax merchant who prided himself on being the town wag, tried to cheer people up with a story of his own: "Once Rabbi Jeremiah ordained a fast and a public prayer, and the rain fell after sunset. The people thought it was due to the merits of the community, whereupon the rabbi replied: 'Let me quote you a parable. This can be compared to a servant who kept begging his master for a special benefit until the master finally said, 'OK, OK, give it to him - just don't let me hear his voice again!'"

A few people chuckled for the sake of politeness, but thereafter a somber silence fell over the crowd. Joseph the butcher, who fancied himself a scholar, looked up from his butcher's block and launched into a complicated argument designed to show off his command of Hebrew.

"Rain is withheld only because of the neglect of the Torah, as it is written: *By slothfulness the rafters sink in.* What is meant by sloth? In Hebrew this is *yimak*, and it refers to the indolence of Israel in not occupying themselves with the words of Torah, as it is written in -"

Adda the fisherman interrupted. "Rain is only withheld because of the sins of violent robbery," he declared, to the general approval of his listeners, who nodded their heads in agreement. "Why just last month, I had no sooner stepped from my boat with the biggest catch I've had in years and those rascals from -"

Here Salla broke in, doubt in his voice. "Rabbi Hamnuna says that rain is withheld only because of the insolent ways of the rich."

"Maybe," Rabbi Ammi suggested, raising his eyebrows in an insinuating kind of way, "maybe the rain is withheld only because the holy laws of impurity are in danger." He looked around to see the reaction. There was a dead silence. Then Rabbi Simon, who had been standing on the rim of the crowd, spoke up quietly and said,

"Rain is withheld only because of those who speak slander, as it is said: *The north wind bringeth forth rain, and a backbiting tongue an angry countenance*." At this, the people looked down shamefaced, and the crowd quietly dispersed. But the damage had been done. And when they passed the house of Chana the Widow, they began looking at it with speculative eyes.

* * *

Whether it was the state of the heavens that filled Rachel with anxiety or the uncertainty over her future, Rachel herself scarcely knew. But one way or the other, that meeting with Issur, that strange and angry meeting, left her feeling more desolate, and more alone, than she had ever felt in her life. She returned home from the market place in a daze, unconscious of anything along the way except the wild confusion that filled her entire being. But no sooner did she step over the threshold than she stopped cold, gripped by a sudden apprehension that almost paralyzed her with fear. Where was the *apakenak*, the beautiful rock crystal that Issur had given her all those years ago? In her mind's eye she saw the way Issur had placed the shimmering rock before her that rainy spring morning, and the delight with which she and Shirin had watched it flash with light, filling the rough-hewn room with all the colors of the rainbow. That rock had been one of the very few things she took with her from home, and so precious to her that she had sewn it deep into her saddle-clothes, away from prying eyes and acquisitive hands. And not once during that caravan journey across the mountains, when the travelers would camp for the night around the fire and tell stories of wild desert bandits and marauding tribes, had she gone to sleep without making sure that that rock of crystal was still safely hidden away. How, then, could it have so completely slipped her mind upon reaching Nehardea? She entered the house and called out to Chana, to Tavi, to Rabbi Strabo, but no one was home.

Returning from the market place a while later, Chana and Tavi were greeted by the sight of cupboards flung wide open in the atrium and strange noises coming from the cellar below the kitchen floor. They heard a loud thud, and then the sound of crates being bumped along the rough stone surface. The two women looked at each other. "It isn't mice," Chana said, and made her way over to the cellar door. "Who's down there?" she called.

Rachel appeared in the opening, her face smudged and dirty but her eyes burning black like fire. "Where are my saddle-clothes?" she asked, rather wildly.

"Rachel, come up here this minute," her aunt commanded. But Rachel just ignored her and repeated with greater emphasis, "Where are my *saddle-clothes*?" and sounded wilder than ever. Tavi peered down at the girl through the cellar door.

"If you're talking about all those grubby blankets you brought with you when you first came to Nehardea," she said, "the ones covered all over with heathen lice and vermin, there's no point in looking for them down there - I burned them long ago."

Rachel gasped. "You burned them?"

Tavi nodded virtuously.

Rachel grew silent, overwhelmed by a sense of guilt and betrayal. In little less than an hour, that rock had grown to enormous proportions in her mind, becoming nothing less than the embodiment of everyone and everything she had ever loved back in Parthia. The sense of loss was overwhelming. To her aching heart, it seemed that it was not only Issur she had betrayed in losing that rock, but her entire past, and the very deepest part of her soul. She came slowly up the stairs, a sorry looking heap of dust and grime. The wildness had gone out of her, and she allowed Tavi to bring an ewer of hot water and to bathe her face and hands. Chana hovered in the background, worried and angry at one and the same time. She had heard some unpleasant tidings out there in the market place, and hurried home to have it out with Rachel. Though she gave no credit to Yalta's insinuations, and was confident that Rachel had only run into an old acquaintance from Parthia, she was furious with Rachel for meeting him "like that" in the streets of Nehardea, and Rachel's attempts at self-defense - "But what was I supposed to do?" or, more defiantly, "What was wrong with it anyway?" - only made her the angrier.

Rachel ran upstairs and shut herself in her room, sick with grief and anxiety. From her window she could see clusters of people huddled outside in the street, and rightly or wrongly she felt sure they were all talking about her. That scene with Issur had shaken her to the very core. To think of Issur turning away from her! It was beyond belief. Issur had been part of her world for as long as she could remember, as ever-present and reassuring as the mountains over their valley. Again and again she went over the scene in her mind, changing now this part of the dialogue and now that, but without being able to escape the overwhelming fact that Issur had parted from her in anger. When, after a while, Chana came upstairs and tried to talk with her through the bolted door, Rachel just said, "Please go away" and buried her face between her knees. Tavi tried to bluster her way in, but soon Rachel heard a resounding slap and then the sound of running steps. Chana's voice came through the door.

"Rachel," she said gently, "Tavi's gone, and she won't bother you any more. Please open the door. I must talk with you." But Rachel just sat by the window and didn't answer, watching the afternoon light fade with unseeing eyes.

But gradually, towards evening, the numbness of grief began ebbing away, and was slowly replaced by a terrible and fearful anxiety. And also, she suddenly realized, by a rapidly growing anger. Was any of this her fault? she found herself telling Issur, growing angrier by the minute. Was she to blame for having been taken from Parthia, or falling in love with the young man they'd picked out for her? Or even - with mounting indignation - that she'd been born in Nehardea in the first place? She felt exhausted by her emotions and conscious of an overwhelming need to have everything settled; to settle everything right away, right now, once and for all. To feel sure of Rami, and of her place in Nehardea. To feel sure that he still wanted her. Only that could ease this sense of being totally alone in the world. If Rami loved her then he should tell her so and marry her now. Show her - show all Nehardea! - that he did not care a fig for her inheritance, and that it was Rachel herself that he wanted. This lack of certainty, this waiting for answers, was as bad as the waiting for rain, and Rachel felt a feverish need for action mounting inside her.

That night, while the household was asleep, she slipped out of her room, unlatched the heavy front door, and ran out into the darkness towards the river. She ran swiftly but even so she was shivering, for she was dressed only in the thin cotton clothes that had covered her when she first came to Nehardea. Before leaving she had taken all her fine clothes - the beautiful linens and silks given her by Chana, the pretty silver bangles bought in the markets of Nehardea - and placed them in a neat pile on her bed. If Rami still wanted her, she would go to him as her, Rachel, without all the finery that rightfully belonged to that other Rachel, Samuel's daughter. As she straightened the bundle she wished, and not for the first time, that she knew how to write. She hated to leave Chana like this, without a word of explanation.

The river banks were quiet at this late hour of the night. The stars gleamed overhead and the moon raced through the clouds. Now that she was no longer running the cold went right through her and she sat huddled between the thick brambles of undergrowth, hugging her arms around her to keep warm.

Despite her anxiety she must have fallen asleep, for gradually she became aware of a sound breaking the silence of the night and dragging her back into consciousness. She stumbled to her feet, shivering with cold.

Down by the marshy reeds of the river bank she glimpsed an old river man tying up his boat, his arms full of ropes and cords, and making his way up the embankment. She ran down to meet him.

"Why, miss," he said, surprised by the young girl who suddenly appeared out of the darkness. "What are you doing out here by yourself? And on a cold night like this."

"Can you take me to Sura?" she asked.

He looked at her with measuring eyes. "Well, I *can*," he said emphasizing the last word. "It's less than twenty parasangs from here, and the current is strong. But I don't know that I should. Why are you going this time of night? You shouldn't be out by yourself."

"But will you take me?" The old man remained silent, measuring her with troubled eyes. Whatever he saw must have changed his mind, for he nodded his head after a minute and retraced his steps back to the river. Silently he helped the girl into the boat, and let the rope slip from its mooring. Within a few seconds Rachel found herself out on the river, the walls of Nehardea receding with every dip of the paddle.

The old man made no attempt to talk, and for this she was grateful. After a while he lay aside the paddle and let the boat skim along with the current. Once again she fell asleep, and when she woke, she was conscious of tears on her face. The old man was watching her sympathetically.

"I know the signs," he said kindly. "Was young once myself. I hope the young fellow's worth it." Rachel smiled and gulped, unable to answer.

"Had a fight, did you?" the boatman asked astutely. "Never you mind. These things happen."

"No, not a fight, exactly," Rachel replied hesitantly, unsure how to reply, but not wanting to snub the kind-hearted old man. The waters carried the boat along in silence.

"Well, if he be a good lad, he'll forgive and forget," the old man said comfortingly after a little while. "Our rabbis teach us that a man should always be gentle as the reed and never unyielding as the cedar. Let me tell you a story. Once, a scholar who had just delivered a brilliant sermon was making his way back home to Tiberias and feeling mighty pleased with himself indeed. On the road he chanced to meet an exceedingly ugly fellow, who greeted him with the words, 'Peace be upon you, sir.' And what did Rabbi Eleazar reply? He said, 'You worthless creature! How ugly you are! Are the rest of your townspeople as ugly as you?'"

"'I don't know,' the man answered. 'Why don't you ask the Craftsman who made me?'"

"When Rabbi Eleazar realized his sin, he got off his donkey and prostrated himself before the man. 'Please forgive me!' he begged. 'I apologize to you.' But the man refused to forgive him, and Rabbi Eleazar followed him all the way to Tiberias, he pleading and the man refusing. When they reached the gates of Tiberias the townspeople saw Rabbi Eleazar and came out to welcome him, saying, 'Peace be upon you, O great teacher.'

Looking around in great perplexity, the other man asked 'Who are you calling a great teacher?'

'Why, the man walking behind you,' they replied. Then the man said, 'If he is a master, may there be no more like him!' And he told them what happened.

'You must forgive him nevertheless,' they replied, 'for he is a great scholar of Torah.'

'Well,' the man sniffed, 'For your sakes I forgive him, but only on condition that he does not make a habit out of such behavior.'

Upon hearing this, Rabbi Eleazar entered the House of Study and preached, 'A man should be pliant as a reed, and not hard as a cedar.'" The boatman chuckled in delight over the story.

Rachel, half frozen in the bottom of the boat, found herself drifting in and out of consciousness and unable to completely follow the boatman's words. Nevertheless, it seemed to her there was something wrong with his story. What had she done that needed forgiving? Again, she felt the anger welling up inside her. Why was she always being made to feel as though she had done something wrong? Why this sense of guilt, and of ever-present shortcomings? Was it her fault that she had an accent, and that the girls laughed at her pronunciation sometimes? Or that she didn't know all the prayers like they did, or the myriad details of synagogue ritual? Or that her heart whispered to the wrong gods at drought? She tried to say some of this to the boatman but found the effort too exhausting. Taking her silence for agreement, the boatman ended his story and repeated once again, "and from this we learn that a man should always be gentle as the reed and never unyielding as the cedar. You'll see," he added kindly, "he'll forgive you."

It was pitch dark when they finally reached Sura. Rachel woke only when the boat scraped against the river bank, and slowly returned to consciousness. She must have been dreaming; wild, half confused images whirled chaotically in her brain. She stumbled when she tried to get out of the boat, and felt confused and dazed. What was wrong with her? Was she sick? She fumbled on her arm to undo the clasp of her silver bracelet, and discovered that her arm was bare. Yes, of course, she had left the bangle with the rest of her things on the bed before she left Chana's house. But when had that been? It seemed like years and years ago. A feeling of despair overtook her. How was she going to pay for the journey?

When the boatman saw her despair, he shook his head. "Don't worry," he said comfortingly. "You'll pay me another time. Now go find your young man." And he shoved his boat off, singing "The watchmen that go about the city found me, to whom I said, 'have you seen him whom my soul loves?"

The boatman's voice drifted back to Rachel from across the water. She was completely alone, and she realized that not only had she not paid the boatman, but she had also taken the canvas sack that was wrapped around her shoulders, and with which he must have covered her as she slept. She sighed, and turned away from the river bank, concentrating with difficulty on the task before her and trying to focus her eyes in the approaching darkness. How was she going to find Rami? Wild images from her dream still swirled in her brain, and though she shivered from the cold wind she felt burning hot. She kept pushing and pulling at the canvas sack, trying to make it comfortable. Finally she cast it away from her.

The city of Sura rose out of the darkness, like Nehardea surrounded by half-dilapidated walls and towering date-palms. The gates were wide open and when she walked in there was nobody in the streets. Shutters were closed, and not a sound issued from any of the houses, not a candle flickered in the windows. Where was everybody? Surely it was too early yet for the whole town to be asleep. In Nehardea the servants would be gossiping together behind the kitchens or in the market-place, free at last from their labors of the day, and the houses of the sages would be bright with the light of oil-lamps, a comforting sign to all passers-by that the study of Torah had not been forsaken and that all was right with the world. But here everything was dark and silent, like a town that had been abandoned.

Rachel walked on, and as she walked she slowly became aware of a strange trumpeting sound, followed by a steady, dull hum. As she drew nearer the sound, the hum changed to a low rumble and then to a positive roar. Turning the corner of the main thoroughfare, she found herself gazing upon a very strange scene indeed.

There, gathered in the open square was what looked to be the entire population of the city. Only, it was clearly no holiday celebration. Everyone - men, women, children, servants - was dressed in sackcloth and completely barefoot. Even the few stray animals - a goat here, a sheep there - were draped in sack. In the middle of the square several men were intermittently blowing the ram's horn - Rachel remembered it from the High Holy Days - and the people were praying in unison. Only, they were not whispering their prayers, but shouting them as loud as they could and their faces were turned upwards, as though straining to see whether the heavens would open up and accept them. Faces were tear-stained and pale. Rachel turned to one young woman and caught at her arm.

"What is going on?" she demanded.

The young woman turned her eyes from Heaven only long enough to see who could possibly be so ignorant, and saw the young stranger.

"*Taᶜanit*," she answered briefly, pulling away from Rachel's grasp and fixing her eyes once again towards the heavens.

The word sounded familiar to Rachel and she strove to remember its meaning. She searched and searched in her memory, but the word eluded her dazed thoughts. She tried to ask the woman what it meant, but she had raised her voice in prayer again and did not reply.

Rachel walked on. The scene frightened her, and pulled her out of the strange lethargy she had felt ever since getting into the boat that evening. Where was Rami? She went from one person to the next in the darkness, peering into the face of each man she met to see if it might be him. No one looked at her or paid her any attention. She tried asking once or twice where he was, but received no response and after a while she stopped asking.

Then she saw him. It might have been hours or it might have been minutes, she herself never knew. But suddenly, from quite a distance away she saw a man, his face turned upward and his eyes closed. His face was hidden in shadows like everyone else, but she knew it was him.

"Rami!" she cried out and ran over. But he didn't turn. "Rami!" she cried again, pleading, and grasped his hand. He looked down for a second, and she saw his eyes flicker with something she couldn't read. He hesitated a moment, and then pulled her away from the crowd. They walked in silence till they reached the river's edge, and Rachel saw his eyes sweeping the banks for a boat.

"What are you doing here?" he asked, and his voice sounded stern. "How in the world did you come?"

"There was a boatman –" Rachel started to explain and then broke off as the words that were crowding her heart spilled over. "There's something I have to ask you," she said, and tried to make her voice as steady as she could. But she was shivering with the cold, and he saw it.

"You're not even dressed properly," he said shortly. "You shouldn't have come."

"But I had to know . . . I mean . . ." Now that the moment had come Rachel didn't know what to say. She felt her face burning with shame, and she was unable to speak the words she had come to ask. "What do you have to know?" he asked, not very gently.

Making an effort to overcome her shivering and to collect her wandering thoughts, she brought out the first words of her question: "Are we . . ." and then broke down. Summoning up all her courage she finally asked, though far less directly than she intended, the question she had come to ask. "Rami, when are we going to marry?"

He sighed impatiently. "I don't know, Rachel, it depends on what the court decides about - well, about several things. You know that."

"But Rami," she pleaded, "We don't *have* to wait for them; we can just go away and marry. We don't *have* to do as they say."

"But I don't want to go against the court," he told her angrily. "I don't want to go against the court *or* my family."

She looked at him. Could she be hearing right? Would he really let others decide their future? Could he really be willing to give her up? She stepped closer to him, wanting terribly to hold him, to put her arms around his body, but there was something about him that froze her in place and kept her from moving. She could no more reach out and touch him, or force him to touch her, than she could bend a piece of iron through the sheer force of her will. There was a long pause and then he turned away from her, fixing his eyes once again on the heavens.

Rachel was stunned. Never had she imagined that this would be his answer. Never had she really believed that he would give her up, and all of a sudden she felt as though a terrible abyss was splitting open before her, ripping through the earth and tearing it asunder, leaving her alone on one side of the pit and all the rest of the world on the other. But what amazed her the most, was that just at this moment when she felt most alone, and when the rest of the world seemed to be slipping rapidly away, it was not Rami whom she saw on the other side of that abyss, and to whom her soul cried out. It was Issur. And it was this sudden insight into her own heart, the knowledge that without Issur the whole world would be as nothing to her, that made her feel as though a giant rock had slammed into her, shattering what was left of her world into a million tiny pieces. She stepped away, and as she did so everything swirled and turned black in front of her eyes. She tried to fight the darkness but it was too much for her, and without a sound she slipped senselessly to the earth.

Chapter Fifteen

The gentle tapping against the window panes grew steadily louder. Rachel gradually became aware that she was awake and lying in bed, but she kept her eyes closed. She knew there was something she had to remember. Slowly, various images began assembling themselves in her mind: the endless journey down the Euphrates with the boatman, the darkness of that strange night, the wailing of strained faces lifted up to heaven. And Rami. The memory of that night came flooding back, and she felt tears trickling beneath her closed eyelashes. And then she heard the rain. She opened her eyes. It was raining heavily, water rushing down the panes of the window through a deep greyish light, softly reflected by the light of a candle. And across from her, Chana was leaning forward, her eyes resting anxiously on the girl's face.

"Where am I?" Rachel asked.

"In Nehardea," Chana said quietly. "You're at home, in your own room. You've had a terrible fever for almost a week now."

"Oh," she said. She sat up cautiously, gingerly testing her arms and legs. "How did I get back?" she asked.

"Your uncle was there in Sura," Chana told her. "He saw you talking to Rami - and a good thing, too. He had gone earlier to Sura to take part in the *ta*ᶜ*anit*. He said it was nearly dawn, when he saw you." There was a long silence while they both listened to the rain beating down. There would be a harvest this year after all, and food and provender for everyone. Rachel knew that she should be glad for this, at least, yet all she could feel was grief; a deep, heavy grief that deadened every other emotion. She remembered, puzzled, the scene that had greeted her eyes in the darkened city, and the way everybody had turned from her.

"What were they doing there?" she asked. "Everyone was dressed in sack cloth, and the whole town seemed to be out there in the market place."

"It was a *ta*ᶜ*anit*," Chana explained. "They were praying for rain."

Of course. *Ta*ᶜ*anit*. That was what that girl had said, out there in the darkness, and the meaning of the word came rushing back to her. Rachel lay back in bed, listening to the rain and recalling every detail of that strange night and of the events leading up to that boat trip down the Euphrates. At last she turned to Chana.

"He turned away from me," she said, almost dragging the words out. But it was not Rami she meant, or of whom she was thinking. Understandably enough, however, her aunt mistook her meaning.

"I know," Chana replied, and then added, with a glimmer of a smile, "Rami told your uncle he didn't know it would make you faint dead away."

"It didn't!" Rachel replied indignantly, swallowing the bait and speaking out in self-defense. "I was sick. I must have been sick ever since I left Nehardea that night, I had been shivering all the way . . . " She stopped as she saw the triumphant glint in her aunt's eyes, and her relief at this show of emotion. Chana, she realized, had been afraid that something had broken her spirit. There was a long silence.

Chana had indeed been afraid. Afraid and angry. Afraid that Rachel might die, and angry that after all her plans to avoid precisely this kind of situation, Rachel had been hurt after all. Why else had she allowed her to become acquainted with Rami before the betrothal, if not to ensure that her heart was given to the right man? And now, precisely because of this caution, learned from the hard lessons of life at Shulamit's sick-bed, Rachel was going to be hurt just like her mother, and perhaps even die. For as Rachel lay on her bed these last few days, often delirious with fever, she could no longer pretend not to know why Shulamit had almost died, in those days after Lajash.

"It isn't fair," Shulamit thought to herself, with more than a little resentment. Some mysterious fate was playing with her well-ordered life, and it simply wasn't fair. "I was only trying to do my best for her - and aren't we supposed to learn from the past? I did everything I could to keep her from being hurt."

Such were Chana's thoughts as she watched over Rachel during those feverish days and nights, just as she had once watched over Rachel's mother. And hence, Rachel's quick show of spirit came to her as an immense relief and a most welcome surprise. Anger and fear slipped away all at once, and sitting up straight, she felt herself becoming her usual practical self.

"Why did you do it?" Chana asked after a while, at her most pragmatic. "What made you go there, at night like that and all alone? Not," she added, with a speculative look at Rachel, "surely not because of the *ta*ᶜ*anit*?" and received a shake of the head in reply.

Indeed, why *had* she gone there? How could Rachel explain the fears and doubts that had been building up inside of her when they were now, somehow, so unimportant? She did her best to explain, to herself no less than to her aunt, but the words came stumblingly and after a while she gave up. Yet Chana listened intently, and did her best to understand.

"Maybe you did want rain," she said at last, thoughtfully, thinking Rachel's words over in silence, and perhaps remembering certain long-ago moments from her own youth. "Maybe you needed rain, too; only, rain of a - of a different kind." She reached over to take Rachel's hand, and the girl suddenly burst into tears; great, gulping tears that threatened to choke her and that looked as though they would never stop. The sound of the rain, of the thundering clouds and crashing lightening, responded to something deep inside of her and loosened her heart. At last, however, the tears subsided and Rachel lay spent and empty, listening to the rain that continued to pour without cease. She lay so quietly that Chana stood up to leave, thinking her asleep.

Rachel opened her eyes. "Are you angry with me?" she asked, somewhat wistfully.

"No," Chana sighed, in a resigned kind of way. "No, of course not." And she leaned over and kissed the girl on her cheek. "I'm just glad you're safe. That's all that matters. Try and sleep now." And blowing out the candle, she left the room.

But Rachel did not go back to sleep. Exhausted though she was by the fever, and though no longer sustained by the tension before it, her mind was lucid and clear, or perhaps she was just too weak to fight the truth any longer. That confrontation with Rami; that moment when Issur had seemed lost to her forever, carried away to the other side of the abyss, had shown her her own heart as never before, and she understood now the true source of the grief to which she had woken. The grief wasn't because Issur had turned away from her in anger; strangely enough, that played a very small role in her thoughts. His turning away was almost incidental to the matter, and, she felt sure, of no lasting consequence. Issur had been angry with her - of course he had been angry; look what she said to him - but she knew that he would come back to find her. To cite this as the source of her grief was only a dodge, a cloak to hide the truth from herself because the truth was almost too painful to bear. The grief wasn't because Issur had turned away from her, but because *she* had turned from Issur. It was she who had repulsed; she who had spoken about loving someone else; and in so speaking had betrayed both Issur and herself in the most fundamental way.

She lay very still, listening to the rain, her thoughts drifting in and out of sleep, when a sudden memory intruded itself onto her consciousness. How odd; it was the memory of something that had occurred years ago, in Parthia; an incident forgotten almost as soon as it happened, and that seemed of no importance at all at the time. Yet now the memory tore at her heart, like a beast of prey that had only been sheathing its claws all these years, waiting for the right moment to pounce. How old was I at that time, she wondered: twelve, thirteen? She counted the years on her fingers. Five years ago, or six at the most. But it had been springtime; of that she was sure . . .

It was springtime, and one morning she and Shirin awoke to the joyous sound of lutes and cymbals, and jumping out of bed they ran to the window and saw a wedding procession winding its way down the valley. Receiving permission from Mother, they ran to join the procession and found that Issur was already there with his friends, together with many other acquaintances from across the valley. The wedding ceremony took place in a high grassy glade surrounded by thickets of oak and juniper, but the children had seen too many such ceremonies for it to hold their attention for long, and they clustered together at the edge of the glade, the boys in one group, the girls in another. The boys seemed to be having a livelier time of it than the girls, for they had improvised some games for themselves and Shirin had looked on enviously. "We'd better think of something to play, too!" she said to the others.

"What?" asked Maneza, and a dozen girls looked on expectantly: one could always count on Shirin to come up with ideas. Words from the marriage hymn floated down to them on the soft spring breeze and mingled with the song of birds and the rustling of leaves.

"Well, since we're at a wedding," Shirin replied, "let's start thinking about our own weddings. In fact - let's pick out our bridegrooms this very day!" Everyone laughed; only Shirin could come up with an idea like that.

"How are we supposed to do that?" Sorhab had asked curiously, while the rest of the girls perked up their ears.

"Like this," Shirin explained. "Mother once told us a story about a princess whose father, the king, gave a feast for the whole kingdom, and he let her choose her

own bride-groom from amongst the guests. And she indicated her choice by filling a cup of wine, and then going up to the man she chose and giving it to him to drink."

"I know that story," exclaimed Sorhab. "Only I heard it differently. It wasn't a cup of wine that she gave him, but rather she put a crown on his head."

"And," said Farangis, who had also heard the story, "she had already fallen in love with him in a dream."

*"**And**," added Sudaba, who was an incurable romantic, "he had fallen in love with her in a dream, too!"*

"Yes, well," Shirin said, dismissing these latter comments and going back to her basic idea, "we don't have a crown, but we can fetch a cup of wine," and she nodded her chin towards the festively laden tables. "Who wants to go first?"

"I will," Rodoba volunteered, and before anyone had time to reply she ran off to the tables, poured herself a goblet of wine, and then, as the others looked on, walked slowly over to where the boys were standing, carefully holding the goblet in both hands lest it spill.

"She's brave!" whispered Maneza. "I wonder who she'll give it to?"

"I'll bet it's Issur," Shirin whispered back, and the other girl nodded. And sure enough, Rodoba went straight up to Issur and gave him the goblet. Issur took the wine Rodoba offered him, a little puzzled, perhaps, by the gesture, but too intent on the game he was playing with the other boys to give it much thought. Only when he heard a burst of laughter from the girls' side of the glade did he realize that he had been tricked in some way.

Shirin then took her turn, and by now the girls were not the only ones watching. The boys, too, had become aware that Shirin was approaching them, goblet in hand, and though they didn't understand the point of the game, they sensed Shirin's mischief at work. All except Rustam, that is, who watched as Shirin walked towards him and waited complacently for her to offer him the goblet. The girls also saw that Shirin was apparently heading towards Rustam, but at the last moment she veered towards Khusrau, the village bully, and graciously gave it to him to drink – much to Rustam's obvious discomfiture. Everyone laughed, and Rustam turned a fiery red.

By now the boys had figured out the game, though just what it portended they didn't know, and they watched as Sudaba ran over to the table, took up a goblet filled with wine, and then, like Shirin, walked slowly over to where the boys were standing. Sudaba appeared to be making straight towards Godarz, and as she approached, the boys hooted loudly and Godarz turned as red as Rustam, and looked as though he wished he could just vanish into the ground. But there was no hope for it, and when Rodoba gave him the goblet, Godarz, somewhat shamefacedly, took a sip.

Throughout all this, she herself had been watching idly, not in the least eager to take her turn with the goblet, and indeed quaking at the mere thought of doing so. But when Shirin began coaxing her all the others followed suit, and she found herself with the goblet in hand before she knew what was happening. She glanced over at Issur, the boy she knew best, and saw that he was looking at her, expecting, indeed wanting her to come to him. Steeling herself, she took a few steps forward and then a few more, but before she was halfway across her trembling hands opened and the goblet shattered to the ground. That was the end of the games that day, and Rachel remembered that they had left the others soon after the incident and gone back home up the mountain. But she had seen the look in Issur's eyes, and she knew that she had hurt him.

Odd that an incident so long forgotten should come back to her now, and come back with such swift and fierce emotion. She cried at what she had done to Issur; cried with the same great choking tears as before, only silently this time, so that no one should hear. No one should ever know what she had done to Issur; no one must ever know how she had hurt him - that would only be to hurt him all over again. Again she saw the look in his eyes. But gradually, very gradually, her tears subsided, and in her heart she felt a resolve stirring strongly to life, and the knowledge that never again would she turn from Issur. And with this knowledge, which brought her a certain measure of comfort and release, she was at last able to fall asleep.

* * *

The storm outside her window ended, and Rachel fell into a deep and comforting sleep that lasted the night through, and removed the last of Chana's worries over her health. It rained gently without stopping over the next few days, and Chana and Rabbi Strabo hovered around the convalescent's bedside, entertaining her with stories and tempting her with delicacies baked especially for her by Tavi ("with nary a grumble," as Rabbi Strabo told her confidentially, apparently much impressed by the fact). Chana could only be grateful that Rachel had recovered and that she no longer cried, and for a few days she forgot all her worries over Rachel's future, content just to have her safe at home. But by the next week the sun was shining, and the rains had stopped, and people were complaining about the puddles and the mud as though there had never been any worry about drought, and court was in session, and Yalta in triumph; and Rachel's loves, and Rachel's properties, were again uppermost in everyone's mind.

Chana returned to Rabbi Nathan's court with renewed purpose and grit, determined to untangle whatever knots had been left dangling in the matter of Rachel's inheritance and to settle Rachel's marriage to Rami once and for all with Rabbi Huna. This would be no easy matter, for those days before the rains had brought out a number of unhealed wounds in the community, and tempers remained raw and uncertain. Old tensions had surfaced; long-simmering disagreements flared into open antagonism. Now more than ever would Chana need all her tact and considerable insight into the minds of her townsmen, and she girded her loins, figuratively speaking, for the last fight ahead. It therefore came to Chana like a bolt out of the blue when Rachel - ungrateful thing! - went into open rebellion at the breakfast table one morning, and declared that she could not marry Rami.

"What do you mean you can't marry Rami?" Chana asked, almost as perplexed as she was angry, for hadn't Rachel been in love with the boy up till now? Not a week ago she had been running after him all the way to Sura, and crying her eyes out because he turned away from her. And now she didn't want to marry him? This was going too far. A girl had the right to reject a marriage proposal, to be sure; but she certainly did not have the right to change her mind about one. She, Chana, had never heard of such a thing! So it was with a good deal of asperity that she asked Rachel again, "What do you mean you can't marry him?"

"I mean that I won't."

Though aggravated almost beyond patience, Chana tried to be reasonable. Perhaps, she said to herself judiciously, perhaps this was all too much for the girl; too soon after her illness and that unfortunate meeting the night of *taᶜanit*. So she subdued her irritation and said as peaceably as she could.

"You mean: you won't marry him now, but that you will later?"

Rachel poured herself some milk. "No, I mean never."

"And why not, pray tell?" Chana could not keep the sarcasm out of her voice, but she realized her mistake the moment she spoke. Rachel flushed as though stung, and her eyes flashed with anger. Recognizing the danger signs, Chana changed tactics.

"Rachel," she said gently, "what's wrong? I thought you loved Rami."

Putting down her cup, Rachel studied the table cloth for a few moments, and then looked back up at her aunt. Her voice was steady. "Maybe I did," she said. "Maybe I did love him at one time - I don't know. When we met, it was as though he came in answer to my prayers. You see, I had been feeling so lonely, and was praying to Hordad, the goddess of the sacred waters, to -"

"You asked a Parthian rain goddess to bring you Rabbi Huna's son?" Chana asked blankly, with a rather dry edge to her tone. But Rachel just gave her a look and went on, her voice a bit more heated now.

"But I do know that I don't love him now, and that I won't marry him." And with that she got to her feet and walked out of the room.

That action, together with the look in Rachel's eyes, completely floored Chana. "How did I ever think she was like her mother?" Chana wondered to herself, startled. Those weren't dreams in Rachel's eyes, those were thoughts: shadows and pools of deep, reflective thought. Those weren't Shulamit's eyes. The discovery rather shook Chana's self-confidence, for she had always prided herself on her powers of judgment. But only for a moment. After a brief hesitation she followed the girl up the stairs, and going into her bedroom shut the door firmly behind them.

"Rachel," Chana asked rather sternly, looking her niece straight in the eyes, "tell me you're not thinking of marrying that man you called a brother back in Parthia - you told me once that you were engaged to him."

"Yes," said Rachel bitterly, "and you told me that I couldn't marry some wild tribesman." There was a long pause; so long that Chana thought that Rachel was not going to say any more. But then she looked up, and to Chana's surprise began speaking in great earnest, apparently doing her best to make her aunt understand.

"I was brought up with Issur. And he loved me. From the very beginning he loved me. Even when other people laughed at me, or looked at me as though I had no right to be there. Yes, and he fought for me, too, and never once asked whose daughter I was, or what dowry I would have if we married. Indeed, he knew I had nothing."

"Well," Chana said gravely, "I am glad that he was so good to you, and it is right that you should feel grateful. But it cannot be right to marry him just because you are grateful, nor could he wish you to so degrade yourself out of sheer gratitude to him and his family."

"But why would it be degrading? Why now, if not then? There were people there who probably thought it would degrade *him* to marry *me*. And any girl there," she added, remembering Rodoba and Maneza and a few others, "would have been glad to have him, but he always chose me."

"But you are Samuel's" - Chana interrupted, trying to put an effective damper on Rachel's argument. But Rachel only became more passionate than ever.

"Samuel's daughter. Yes, I know, but what good did that ever do me? It meant nothing to anyone there, even if they had known. But Issur was the son of Kovad, a warrior from the line of kings and heroes, and the owner of his own fields and pastures, while I - I was the daughter of a strange people from a far away land. What would I have been without him, or without Shirin?"

Chana remained silent for a few moments, at a loss to deal with a situation so utterly beyond all her experience. That Rachel should refuse to marry the son of the Chief Judge of Sura was one thing, but that she should long for a Parthian soldier was quite another.

"Surely," she said to Rachel, and her voice was a mixture of apprehension and disbelief, "surely you don't wish to go back to Parthia? Now that you've come back, could you really leave?"

This made Rachel pause. There had been times, this past week, when that had been exactly what she wanted; when, lying in bed in the days after her illness, there was nothing she wanted more than to go back to Parthia and find everything just as she left it. But now that Chana had actually broached the question, she knew, once and for all, that there was no going back. Too much had changed; *she* had changed. Though Nehardea still seemed foreign to her at times, and the people incomprehensible more often than not, it was home. Even after all those years it had echoed in the forgotten corners of her memory, softening the edges of all that was foreign and making much that was new seem right and familiar. The Sabbath melodies went to her very soul, as did certain prayers in the synagogue. Rabbi Strabo had taught her to read, and the square black letters on the smooth yellowed scrolls had become very precious to her. With halting words, Rachel tried to tell Chana some of this, and to explain what she felt.

Chana nodded with satisfaction at what she heard, tangled though it was and more than a little disjointed. "You mean," she asked Rachel, "that you recognize that Judaism is better than Zoroastrianism? Well, I'm glad you realize that. Indeed, I'd always wondered how the Persians could think as they did, what with all those gods and demons and those strange ideas about - "

But here Rachel interrupted her. "No," she said firmly. "No. It's not a matter of being better. It's not better - and it's not worse. It's just that it's *mine*." And then, while Chana was still trying to digest this, Rachel added with a certain finality: "And I'm not going to marry Rami" - and her tone left no room for argument. So Chana prudently decided to end the conversation on that note, trusting to time, if not her own efforts, to weave together all the loose ends in Rachel's return to Nehardea and the bosom of her family.

Chapter Sixteen

Except for the rains, which now fell as though there had never been any danger of drought, everything continued pretty much as it had before. The trial over Rachel's inheritance continued, the girls looked at her wide-eyed when she joined them after synagogue or came across them in the market place, and Tavi continued to scold. In fact, she scolded so much that Rachel finally lost her temper.

"Why does she dislike me so?" she asked Chana bitterly, after an unusually sharp tongue-lashing one day. "I'm no less Jewish than she is, even if I did grow up in the Gurgan Valley."

"Oh, Tavi's not Jewish," Chana said lightly.

"She's not Jewish?" Rachel gasped. Chana nodded. "Then why is she always scolding me for doing things wrong?"

"She's not Jewish," Chana explained, "but she probably knows as much Jewish law as any woman in Nehardea. You see, her people come from the kingdom of Adiabene and were known as 'God-fearers', like many of the people there, but strictly speaking they're not Jewish, because they never actually converted."

"Good heavens," Rachel said weakly, not knowing whether to laugh or to cry. "From all her scolding, you'd think she was the only Jew in town." She pondered the matter in silence, and then asked thoughtfully, "Can anyone convert?" And it was this question, so ostensibly innocent, that gave Chana the first inkling as to the direction Rachel's thoughts were taking. So Chana adjusted her explanation accordingly, enumerating the rabbinic laws governing conversion to Judaism (and perhaps adding a few of her own making), with an emphasis on details and problems, and plenty of them. Rachel listened attentively, nodding her head throughout the whole thing, though still rather nonplussed by what she'd learned about Tavi.

Thus, in some way, everything remained the same. But in other ways, everything was different. For one thing, Rachel no longer thought about Rami, or if she did it was with indifference; that abyss she had imagined the night of *ta*ᶜ*anit* had carried him far away indeed. Nor did she pay the slightest attention to the judgments in court, or to her aunt's negotiations with Rabbi Huna. On the other hand, her days were now filled with lessons with Rabbi Strabo - and it was not from the scrolls of Herodotus and Strabo that they studied. She made him teach her the Bible, and the meaning of the Hebrew prayers, and to read out loud with correct pronunciation. Chana often found them sitting together over the Scrolls of Law, and smiled with satisfaction at the sight. But one day she found them reading from the Book of Genesis, studying the weekly Bible portion in which Shechem, the pagan prince of Hamor, agreed to become circumcised for love of Dinah, the daughter of Jacob and Leah. Rachel gave her aunt a cheerful smile as she came into the room and said, "Well, I now see why some people convert!"

Chana sighed, not in the least amused by Rachel's acquisition of knowledge, or at least, not amused by her acquisition of this particular piece of it. "You *had* to teach her Bible," she reproved her brother, shaking her head with a chagrin that was not assumed. She sat down at the table and took a good look at her niece. In some subtle way, Rachel had changed during these last few weeks. There was more purpose in her brow, and a new consciousness in her glance. Chana sighed again. She sensed new troubles ahead.

"Yes," said Rachel, very seriously, "we study the Bible portion every week. And the next thing I want to learn, is how to write."

"An excellent idea!" Rabbi Strabo exclaimed, immediately envisioning new copies of all the ancient geographers. But here Chana drew the line.

"Nice Jewish girls don't write," Chana said primly, knowing exactly how Rachel was going to react to that axiom of Jewish tradition. And indeed Rachel sat bolt upright in protest. "But, Aunt Chana, Doneg can write, and she's the nicest girl in Nehardea - even if Yalta *is* her mother."

"Yes," Chana replied, "that's just it; Yalta *is* her mother, and you can be sure that she keeps a close eye on whatever Doneg does!"

Rachel registered this silently; Chana had a point. But then she said, eyes wide open, "But Aunt, *you* can write!"

"I?" said Chana, flabbergasted.

Rachel nodded. "Of course. I've seen you sign documents ever so often."

"Ahh," Chana answered demurely, "but you see, I don't actually sign my name; just make the family mark; like this:" and leaning over the table, she picked up Rabbi Strabo's stylus, dipped it into the ink, and drew a quick date-palm with sprawling fronds. Rachel studied the sketch, and picking up the stylus in turn, drew a rather shaky but still very creditable looking palm tree.

"There!" Chana said, smiling. "Now you can do as much as I can!"

"I still want to learn how to write," Rachel said.

"So that you can send letters to your Parthian?" Chana retorted.

Rachel's eyes twinkled mischievously. "Don't worry," she assured her aunt. "He wouldn't be able to read them."

Chana got up and made for the door. "You're not going to be writing anybody," she said in her firmest way. "And that's that." But when Chana wasn't looking, Rabbi Strabo gave her a distinctly conspiratorial wink, and Rachel knew that he would teach her to write.

* * *

About three weeks after Rachel's late night journey down the Euphrates, the case concerning her inheritance drew to a fairly successful close, and this gave Chana the courage to broach the question of marriage once again. There had been no discussion of the subject since the rather heated argument that night soon after Rachel's illness, and Chana was cautiously optimistic that Rachel would yet agree to marry Huna's son. Surely she had gotten over her little fit of pique that night of *ta^canit*? Or was Rachel still secretly dreaming of her Parthian? It was impossible to tell; if only she could see inside the girl's head! She was reluctant to ask her outright, telling herself that this might do more damage than good. "If there *are* any embers left smoldering," she reasoned, "best to let them go out by themselves." Surely they would never see or hear of this Issur again, and with time - hopefully not too much of it - Rachel would forget these notions and marry Rami and consolidate her position in Babylonia once and for all. So, at least, Chana hoped. But when she finally ventured to reopen the subject, Rachel's response was not encouraging. Unlike the previous discussion, which had called forth such passionate feeling, Rachel now replied with what seemed to her aunt like mild amusement - and that was not a good sign. Looking up from the scroll over which she and her uncle were huddled, she listened politely to all that Chana had to say - and Chana had plenty to say - and then remarked, a propos nothing at all,

"I've been thinking: it's just like in the Bible! Jacob waited fourteen years for Rachel, and Issur waited about the same amount of time for me, more or less - and my name's Rachel, too!"

There was no arguing with that. So Chana tried another angle; if reason didn't work, perhaps shame would. "Here you are," she said to Rachel, shaking her head very sadly, "Here you are: the daughter of the former Chief Judge of Nehardea, one of the greatest scholars of the Jewish people, and you want to link your destiny with a man who can't even read. And you such a fine scholar yourself!" Chana looked pointedly at the scrolls on the table before her, and then at Rabbi Strabo, who had paused while Chana was speaking.

Rachel nodded, perfectly in agreement. "Yes," she said, "I've been thinking about that, too. And it reminded me of what the sages say about Rabbi Akiba, for *he* became the greatest Jewish scholar of all time, even though he only started studying at the age of forty! And it was all due to his wife, and *her* name -"

"Was Rachel, too," said Chana, in her driest tone. "Yes, I know."

Rachel gave Chana an impish grin, and looked with satisfaction from her aunt to her uncle and then back again.

"You know," she said, "I'm really beginning to like my name."

* * *

It was also around this time that Rachel met an elderly gentleman named Avlet, a Persian scholar of the Zoroastrian religion and an old friend of her father's. He came to the house to see her, having recently returned from a long journey to India and been informed that Samuel's daughter had returned during his absence from captivity. Avlet was an aristocratic looking man with finely chiseled features and burning black eyes. His bearing was tall and commanding, and he was dressed Hindu-style in richly patterned brocade and silk; the double-knotted cord of the Zoroastrian, the *kusti*, wrapped around his waist. A well-dressed slave, and a well-behaved weasel of some sort, both with golden collars, waited for their master outside the door of the house. Avlet did not speak much, but just listened with grave interest to everything Chana had to say of Rachel's studies, and of her quick interest in books and learning. He did not ask her about her past, and did not inquire about her future. But when he got up to leave, he put his hand under the girl's chin, tilted her face upwards, and looked deeply into her eyes. "She is truly Samuel's daughter," he pronounced, and for the first time since coming to Nehardea, the words filled Rachel with pleasure.

Chapter Seventeen

Now that the drought was over, Nehardea settled into winter and into winter's cares and activities. Not the least of these was the festival of Hanukkah, or the Festival of Lights, as it was also called, and since this was Rachel's first Hanukkah in Nehardea, Chana explained the festival to her in considerable detail, as she always did at the approach of every new holiday.

"There are eight days of Hanukkah," Chana explained, "for when the Greeks entered the Temple -"

"The Temple in Jerusalem?" Rachel asked, and Chana nodded her head. "So when the Greeks entered the Temple -"

"But what were the Greeks doing in Jerusalem in the first place?" Rachel asked.

"Well," Chana conceded, "actually it was the Syrians, you see, because Alexander the Great - well, never mind for now; get your uncle to explain it to you." And she continued on with her lesson.

"So when they entered the Temple they defiled everything, including the oils used to light the Holy Lamp. But Judah Maccabee and his brothers prevailed against the Greeks, that is, against the Syrians - oh, never mind - and drove them out of Jerusalem. Now, of course, they had to rededicate the Temple and make it fit for divine worship, but when they searched the shelves they found only one cruse of oil fit to light the Holy Lamp. This was enough to keep the light going for only one day, but a miracle occurred, and during the whole eight days that it took for someone to run and bring another flask of oil, the light continued to burn. Thus the rabbis decreed these eight days a festival in which we celebrate this miracle." Chana glanced at Rachel out of the corner of her eye to see if she had any more objections to make to the story, but Rachel was silent, apparently contemplating the miracle of the oil. And Chana sighed in relief. Ever since Rachel had begun studying in earnest she was wont to ask awkward questions, but this lesson seemed to have gone smoothly enough.

The next night was the first night of Hanukkah. The first candle on the eight-branched candelabra was lit, and throughout Nehardea the windows of Jewish homes were flickering with light. And from these same windows came the sound of song and laughter as the Jews rejoiced over the redemption of their people in a place so far away and in a time so long ago. The House of Study adjoining the synagogue was also humming with activity and the earnest discussion of Hanukkah laws, when all of a sudden Rabbi Dimi burst into the room, disheveled and overwrought, and exclaimed, "The *mobad*s are removing the candles!" And then Rabbi Joshua burst into the room with the same tidings, and Joseph the butcher, and Rabbi Kattina the flax merchant, and Adda the fisherman, and Abin the carpenter, until a goodly portion of Nehardean householders were clamoring away in noisy confusion.

The sexton rapped for order and the room fell silent. "Will one of you," he asked, "be good enough to explain yourself?"

Rabbi Dimi stepped forward. "It's the *mobad*s," he said, "the priests of those Zoroastrian fire-temples. They're going around to each house and removing the Hanukkah lights from the windows, calling them a blasphemy to the Zoroastrian gods!"

Again there was a babble of voices, and again the sexton rapped on the table for order, this time to no avail. But no matter; everyone understood perfectly well even without explanations. The Jews of Babylonia had not lived under Persian rule for so many years without having weathered a few storms along the way, especially during the reign of Ardashir, the first of the Sasanian kings. None of these storms, however, had ever really affected Jewish life in Babylonia or created any lasting impact. King Shapur, who followed Ardashir, had been a good king, strong and tolerant of the many religions that flourished in his kingdom. But the roll of dynasty was a chancy business, and a new king of Persia had just been crowned. Hormizd was young and untried, and would be surrounded by counselors of all kinds, all of them jostling for their own interests. Might this not be a chance for the more zealous amongst them to assert their voices? Thus went the conversation that first night of Hanukkah in Nehardea, as the Jews discussed the dangers of the new situation, hoping for the best but fearing the worst.

Rachel was as surprised as anyone by this turn of events. This, her first Hanukkah in Nehardea, had been spent with Doneg at her home, for the two girls had become close friends over the past few weeks. Now that Rachel was no longer to marry Rami, Yalta and Rabbi Nachman beamed at her with good will, and had only smiles for she whom only lately they had done their best to humiliate and impoverish. But Rachel didn't care. Ever since that night of *ta^canit*, she had come to realize what was truly important to her, and Yalta's machinations did not rank high on her list.

Doneg's home was large and impressive, a true Persian *apadna* with an elegant roofed courtyard lined with white columns on three sides of the room, and beautiful gardens and orchards stretching as far as the eye could see. Peacocks strutted amongst the rose-bushes, and the trees were laden with peaches and apricots. A long table was set in the courtyard for dinner; for winters in Nehardea were not generally harsh, and the last few days had been unusually mild. Against the wall there gleamed a silver candelabra with eight calyx-shaped holders in which a single candle burned brightly. "Olive oil," Yalta explained. "Very expensive, of course, but it gives the clearest light. Your aunt uses poppy-seed oil, I believe?" And with that, passed Rachel on to her husband.

Rabbi Nachman seated Rachel next to him at the table, solemnly telling her that he had been Samuel's most devoted student and lamenting that Rachel had never known her honored father. This was followed by a sigh, and then, apparently feeling that he had done his duty, launched into a history of Hanukkah and the events that had led to this night's celebration. Rachel listened politely to his version of the brave deeds performed by the Maccabees against the cruel Grecian ruler of Syria, only adding her voice when a significant pause in the lecture, and a lifting of bushy eyebrows, told Rachel that Rabbi Nachman expected a response of some sort. "And that is why we celebrate Hanukkah," Rabbi Nachman said, winding up his talk with a flourish.

"I wonder," Rachel mused, speaking out of turn, as it were, for there had been no lifting of eyebrows to sanction her temerity, "I wonder if such a thing could ever happen again? That is, a repression like that. Here in Babylonia, for instance."

And now the bushy eyebrows lifted in earnest, for Rabbi Nachman was amazed that anyone should ask such a question. Surely Rachel had been long enough in Nehardea to see how important he was? He cleared his throat. "Here in Babylonia?" he said, his voice signaling his disbelief. "When the Jews are so highly connected to the king and his court? Certainly not. Why, my own father-in-law, the Exilarch, and I myself . . ." but here his voice drifted off modestly. He shook his head with great firmness. "Who would dare to lift a hand against us?" he asked, drawing himself up in righteous indignation at the very thought of it.

The Hanukkah celebrations were at their height when one of the household servants stepped up to Rabbi Nachman and whispered some words in his ears. The Zoroastrian temple-priest was waiting in the ante-room, and soldiers on horseback were standing guard outside the door. Rabbi Nachman rose to his feet in protest, but none of his blustering did any good. The *mobad* entered Rabbi Nachman's mansion just as he had entered other Jewish homes that night, and going up to the *menorah* flickering in the window, calmly removed the lamp and brought it inside the room, setting it down on the table where it couldn't be seen from the street. And then, with a polite bow, left the house. That ended the festivities for the night.

As Rachel walked home from Doneg's house, accompanied by two of Yalta's maidservants, she noticed the darkened windows along the way and wondered if the *mobads* had been to her home, too, and what Chana would have to say about it. Indeed she felt more than a little anxious, and walked back as quickly as she could. But when she got home, Tavi opened the door to her with a look that was more than unusually ungracious, and looked as though nothing would give her greater pleasure than to slam the door in her face.

"*Now* what?" Rachel asked herself, half amused and half angry at being welcomed home in this fashion. But the moment she entered the atrium, she understood. There were two soldiers in the room, both of them loosely covered in chain-mail, with plumed helmets pushed back from their heads; and both of them making polite conversation with Chana and Pazi, who had apparently come a-visiting. A veritable arsenal of weapons was piled high in the corner in a glittering heap: javelins and daggers, long swords and short swords, leather quivers braced in silver and feather-tipped arrows cast in iron. Pazi was looking at the soldiers wide-eyed with admiration, and Rabbi Strabo, who seemed scarcely less charmed, gazed at them with the look of a man who has nothing left to wish for, and planning, no doubt, a new chapter for his great history. And then one of the soldiers rose to his feet and looked at Rachel, a question in his eyes.

"Issur!" she cried out. And this time there was no hesitation. Issur caught her in his arms as she ran up to him, and neither Chana's efforts to separate them nor Tavi's loud-spoken disapproval could make her let him go, or keep them from exchanging their first and long, loving kiss.

* * *

Hanukkah passed, the *mobad*s disappeared back into their fire-temples, and once again Rachel was the topic of conversation throughout Nehardea as news of "her Parthian" spread through the town, courtesy of Pazi, no doubt. But this time Rachel was not around to hear the gossip, and neither Chana's remonstrances, nor Tavi's grumblings, nor the market-place consternation fell on the right pair of ears. One morning soon after Issur's first visit to her home, Chana awoke to find Rachel gone, a neatly-written note on her bed informing her that she and Issur had gone off to marry; a polite post-script referring her to the story of Dinah and Shechem, Genesis 34. Love, Rachel.

"Cheeky thing!" Chana thought resentfully, reaching that post-script, and she crumpled the note in dismay. So this was the end of all her plans! The end of Samuel's seed in Babylonia, the end of all she had worked for this past year; the end of all her hopes! Her sense of failure ran deep, and she was bitter, bitter indeed, against Rachel. She wondered if she would ever see her niece again, or if she even wanted to. No doubt the two of them would trot back to Parthia and live happily ever after amongst the cows and the fire altars. Well, so be it.

But as it turned out, Chana was left with very little time for feeling bitter. Over the course of the next few weeks, events occurred that made even the elopement of Samuel's daughter pale in significance. For it soon became evident that those startling events that first night of Hanukkah were no passing storm, but rather an omen of the great evil to come. There rose to power a priest named Kartir, who knew not Samuel, nor Rav, nor even, as it turned out, the all-powerful Rabbi Nachman. He cared nothing for the traditional alliance between the throne and the Jews, or for the Jewish dignitaries who had always brought such peace and prosperity to their fellow-religionists in Babylonia. Nor was his hand against the Jews alone. Once again royal messengers gathered in the market place, this time to read Kartir's proclamation against all non-Zoroastrians; and across the lands of the vast Persian Empire, Christians, Jews, Buddhists, Brahmins and Zandiks all became the target of Kartir's wrath.

The situation was grave indeed. The Jewish citizens of Nehardea discussed this troubling new development at home and in synagogue, in the streets and the market place, in the shops and the courts, and indeed wherever they met. There were those who lifted their eyes towards other lands and spoke of leaving in good time for Egypt, or Cyrene, or the land of Israel, and the best ways of transferring their wealth. Others, more optimistic, or perhaps less far seeing, spoke of weathering the storm and waiting for better times to come, comforting each other with stories of previous persecutions that had come to naught, and reminding themselves that the miracle of Purim had been wrought in this very land of Persia. Jews who lived next door to each other but had not spoken together for years now met and discussed the new Haman as though nothing had ever divided them. Sages who had spent the last few weeks raking up grievances and accusing each other of various sins now forgot to be angry, and once again exchanged greetings. Even Yalta and Chana were to be seen consulting together in the market place. Yalta had been one of the first to deplore Rachel's elopement with "her Parthian," as she put it, and certainly the loudest in professing her horror that Samuel's daughter, alas, should come to such an end. And to think that only a few weeks ago she, Yalta, had entertained the ungrateful girl in her own home. But now, Yalta was so frightened by the rise of Kartir, so grave and disturbed over these troubling developments, that Chana believed that even were Rachel to suddenly reappear in Nehardea, arm in arm with said Parthian, Yalta would scarcely notice her presence.

Chana also underwent a change of heart and forgot that she had ever been angry with Rachel. She missed her niece and worried about her, and wondered, with more than a pang of anxiety, just how she and Issur were faring. No doubt Issur had captured his fair share of booty these last few months in the service of the King, but surely that wouldn't last forever. Her anxiety was compounded by that reference to Dinah and Shechem in Rachel's letter: just how far did she mean to take that old story? Did Issur really intend to convert to Judaism? Chana had nothing against converts in principle, and in point of fact conversion now seemed to her the best, the only possible solution given Rachel's determination to marry this boy. Unless Rachel returned to Parthia with Issur, that is, but somehow Chana doubted this would happen. She thought that Rachel was too rooted now in Nehardea, and in all that Nehardea symbolized for her - family, religion, ties with the past - to just pick up and leave, as though it had never happened. But if Issur converted to Judaism, that would be problematic as well. Since the rise of Kartir it had become dangerous to convert from Zoroastrianism to any religion at all, dangerous and illegal, as more than a few converts had learned to their grief. So along with her fears for Rachel, Chana was also concerned for Issur, and this went a long way in creating the change of heart that she soon admitted without reservation to anyone who asked how she was taking the whole thing; and there were many who did ask, and not only out of spite, like Yalta. To her dismay, the only person who didn't ask was Rachel herself, for Rachel did not return and the weeks dragged by without a sign from her niece.

* * *

Avlet, the Persian scholar who had been Samuel's friend, was a great traveler, but in between his journeys to the east he dwelt in a small house, richly furnished, on the shores of the Royal Canal just outside Nehardea. One night, while he was sitting late in his study, poring over the scrolls which he had recently brought back from his travels, his servant knocked on the door and informed him that a young couple stood on his doorstep and wished to speak with him. Surprised by the unexpected visitors, he tied his heavy silken robe more firmly around his waist, and picking up his candle wondered who could possibly have come to his house like this, so late at night and unbidden. Entering the atrium, he held his candle high and the light fell on the countenance of the girl he recognized as Samuel's daughter, the young girl they called Rachel. A handsome, dark-haired man of soldierly bearing stood beside her.

Over cake and wine in his scroll-lined study, Issur and Rachel told the elderly savant that they had married, while Avlet stroked his chin and listened, his mien thoughtful and non-judgmental. He was not surprised by the tale, for, like everyone else in Nehardea he had heard about Rachel's elopement, and he had, moreover, received a first-hand account of it from Chana herself. Rachel had warmed to Avlet during his brief visit to Chana's house, and instinctively felt that this grave Iranian who had been her father's friend understood her, and saw more clearly into her heart than anyone else. She was glad that she had followed the impulse that made her seek him out, and soon found herself talking with Avlet as freely as though she had known him all her life. Issur also warmed to the elderly scholar, and together they told him their story, beginning from the beginning, in Parthia. Issur told Avlet about the little girl his father had brought home from the wars, and Rachel told him about her life back in Parthia, and how lonely and out of place she had felt there, despite the affection of her family. She told him of the *gosan*'s song and the mysterious pearl and how it had caused her to think that the answers to her questions lay outside her own valley.

"I asked people about the pearl, quoting what I could remember from the song, and everyone had different ideas. Everyone tried to define it in different ways. I was sure, however, that it had to do with something inside of myself, and that it was something which I alone could find. And I was sure - oh, so sure! - that when I came to this new place, everything would be different. And, indeed, it *was* different - but not in the ways that mattered, somehow. Oh, people dressed differently, and their houses were certainly not like ours, nor their ways of life, and yet it was all very much the same. I still felt lonely and out of place, and I still felt uncomfortable with the people around me. I had the same feeling of disappointment that I did as a little girl, when I would look in the mirror every morning to see if my curls had disappeared during the night. Only, they never did," she exclaimed with a little smile, running her hand through those curls in wry proof of this statement. Avlet smiled a bit, but his eyes remained intent on her face. Issur straightened in his chair, and with an effort kept himself from reaching out and stroking those curls.

"The brushing didn't help much," she conceded, with a smile. "But I began to think that if Nehardea was a mirror reflection of Parthia, at least as far as my own experience of it went, it was because I was seeing *myself* in that mirror, and not the world around me. I knew it was I who had to change, only I didn't know how. But then I became interested in learning about Judaism, and my uncle began teaching me the Bible and the Hebrew language, and my aunt taught me to understand the prayers. And suddenly, almost without realizing it, those other things didn't matter any more. Or at least, they didn't matter as much. Now if one of the girls was a bit cruel, or Tavi scolded me, or someone laughed at me for not knowing something, or for speaking with an accent - it didn't really matter. It didn't make me feel broken in the way that these things used to make me feel, both here and in Parthia."

Avlet looked up keenly at these words. "I remember your father once said to me, that one who studies the Torah is like a great tree, deeply rooted, that stands firm even when all the winds of the world come to blow it away." Avlet thought this over, and then added with a little smile, "It was certainly true of your father, as it is for many of your great sages. Yet, I also believe that it is true for anything that people really believe in." Rachel nodded her head, and after a short silence resumed her tale.

"But my story doesn't end there," she said, looking up at Avlet. "And what makes it so paradoxical is that my interest in Judaism began *after* I realized that I . . . that I loved Issur, and that I . . . that I didn't want to live without him," and here she glanced at her husband, and gave him a shy, loving look. "And isn't that odd?" she asked, finishing her tale and looking up at Avlet with questioning eyes. "It would have made everything so much easier just to marry a rabbi's son, as my aunt wanted, and leave Parthia behind me once and for all, in every way. Yet in the end, it just couldn't be."

But Avlet shook his head. "Odd?" he mused. "Perhaps not. The whole world is a paradox and made up of opposites. Good with evil, night with day," and he quoted softly from the sacred Zoroastrian texts: "From whom is goodness, from whom badness? From whom light, and from whom darkness? From whom fragrance, from whom stench? From who justice, and from whom injustice? From whom compassion, from whom pitilessness . . ." Both Rachel and Issur listened intently to Avlet, as he recited the words familiar to them since childhood.

"We, too, that is, the human part of creation, have a share in this duality. It's because of this very duality," he continued, "that some of us wear the double-knotted cord," and he nodded towards the *kusti* which both he and Issur wore, knotted around the waist in the fashion of Zoroastrians. "And that double-knot, as both of you know, is not so easily untied."

Rachel listened to his words, an arrested expression on her face. Issur smiled a little, as though he too liked the idea. "That's true," Rachel said thoughtfully. "I remember, when I was little, how I always feared that moment when Mother and Father untied the cord at prayer-time, and was afraid of - oh, I don't know what! - of the house catching fire, of the mountains falling down, or who knows what exactly. And then, that sense of relief when the cords were finally retied, double-knotted front and back, and the feeling that all was right with the world."

Avlet's servant entered with a discreet knock to replenish the flagons of wine, and silence reigned in the beautiful, candle-lit room. Issur helped himself to some cake.

"Is my aunt angry with me?" Rachel asked finally, breaking the silence after a few minutes. Her voice sounded wistful and shy.

"Well," Avlet answered thoughtfully, "I believe she *was* rather angry, at first. Just a little, you understand. But now, you know, this situation with Kartir makes everything different, and I believe that her only thought would be relief to have you and your charming husband" - and here he made a slight bow towards Issur - "safely back home." Avlet paused for a moment, and taking a sip of wine continued his discourse.

"Nor do I think that Tavi will be scolding you too much either, this time. In fact, Chana told me that she was ecstatic at the whole thing: said she knew you were a heathen all along!" Rachel laughed a little at this, as Avlet had intended, and some of the tension went out of her face.

"No," he went on, in his most judicial tone of voice, "I don't think anyone at home is really angry with you - apart from Rabbi Strabo, that is: he says you left him high and dry in the middle of chapter three!" And at this all three of them laughed out loud.

"What did you and my father used to talk about?" asked Rachel curiously, with a winning smile. "Philosophy? Religion? Indeed I, too, have noticed so many similarities between Judaism and Zoroastrianism! Little things, perhaps, though not always, and sometimes very beautiful. Like that phrase about Ohrmazd 'wearing the sky as a garment' - you know the one, Issur? - I heard the very same phrase once in synagogue, at the morning service. Not, of course, about Ohrmazd, but still, the very same phrase! And there are so many other things . . ."

Avlet looked attentively at Rachel, liking her words and her enthusiasm, but nevertheless he shook his head in the negative. "No, your father and I never discussed religion at all, or philosophy either, at least not in the accepted sense. We talked about other things: astrology and the stars, and often about medicine. Samuel gave me more than a few good recipes for various treatments and creams, and he knew so much about the stars and their watches that he once told me - I think in all seriousness! - that he knew the face of the heavens as well as he knew the alleys of Nehardea." Avlet took a sip of wine, and then looked mischievously at his guests, a youthful look that sat oddly well upon his stern and ascetic features. "Though I have to confess," he told them, "that one of his precious ointments nearly made me blind for a week! And he may have known the heavens, but by the fire of Ohrmazd, he surely was at a loss in Nehardea - I never knew one for getting so lost on his own street!"

Rachel laughed and this, but then expressed her surprise that her father had found so much to interest him in the realms outside Jewish law and study.

"Well, everyone and his own double-knot," Issur remarked, and Avlet looked at the young man with respect.

It was late when they stood to go, and Avlet spoke a few words in parting. "In the interest of symmetry," he said, smiling at Rachel, "I really should give you a pearl as a wedding present," and Rachel knew that he was referring to the *gosan*'s song, "but I think that would be a rather trite end to your quest." Avlet paused. "But no matter; I also think you're going about your quest perfectly well on your own, without my help." He gave Rachel his hand. It was the hand that had touched her father's, and as she touched its palm she was deeply moved. With a final blessing for them both, Avlet retreated into his study and the servant closed the door behind them.

The cold wind came as something of a shock after the warmth and light of Avlet's home, and all at once, the optimism, the quiet confidence with which that meeting had inspired them, dissolved into the winter night as though it had never existed at all. The symbolism of the *kusti,* so beautifully apt back there in that candle-lit study, now seemed little more than a childish attempt, pitifully inadequate, to express the forces that had brought them to wed, and that would be needed to keep them together. For her, Rachel knew, it would be easier: Nehardea was her home and the Jews were her people. But for Issur? Everything would depend on his love for her, for it was that alone which had brought him to this point. It was a great gift, this love of Issur's, but it was also a terrible responsibility, and it frightened and humbled her at one and the same time. And all of a sudden, she didn't think it would be so easy for her after all.

Issur and Rachel stood facing each other, reading their questions in each other's eyes, and neither of them speaking a word. But then Issur brought her hand to his lips and kissed the closed fingers, and Rachel brushed the back of her hand against the roughness of his cheek. And as they went on their way, on a path made dim and uncertain by the darkness of the night and the thick, scudding rain clouds, Rachel opened her hand and found herself holding a ring of gold, beautifully chased and obviously ancient, from which there gleamed a diamond of great purity and inestimable value.

Epilogue

In the end, things fell out just as Avlet predicted. When Rachel and Issur finally knocked at her aunt's door, as they did very soon after that visit to Avlet, Chana and her uncle were not the only ones who greeted the runaways with a sigh of relief. Indeed, the entire Jewish community came out to welcome them. Kartir's shadow was lying heavily on Nehardea these days, and the Jews closed ranks as though there had never been any arguments to divide them, or harsh words and accusations to drive them apart. Harmony and peace was the order of the day within the community itself, since there could be none outside of it. Samuel's daughter was welcomed back with open arms. Issur even became something of a hero in the eyes of many Jews for having converted under such difficult circumstances, and for coming under the wings of the Divine Presence at a time when Judaism was fallen into disgrace, and Kartir seeking to destroy the Jews, root and branch. Thus it came to pass that although Rachel and Issur married in such . . . such biblical fashion, as it were; without ring, or canopy or blessing; and although their son Mari was conceived before Issur formally converted, Mari was good enough to delay his birth till his father could convert to the very letter of Jewish law. Or, as the sages put it: "Though the conception of Rachel and Issur's son was not in holiness, his birth *was* in holiness." And so it must have been indeed, for Samuel's grandson, the son of Rachel and Issur the Convert takes his place amongst the sages of the Babylonia Talmud, from whence he peeks out at us to this very day.

CPSIA information can be obtained
at www.ICGtesting.com
Printed in the USA
BVOW03s1301150817
492122BV00001B/4/P